"Why are you ... What have I done?"

Cressida could no longer tolerate the intensity of Luke's gaze. Anger blazed her to life. "You're looking at me as though I was something you wouldn't wipe your feet on. Why? Because I was in the company of another man? Does it amuse you to treat me this way?"

"I've seldom been less amused," was Luke's level reply.

"Then what is the matter with you?" Cressida nearly screamed. "Why are you sulking?"

Suddenly Luke's restraint was banished by her careless words. His eyes were filled with fire as he reached out and pulled Cressida into the hard, fierce tension of his body.

"I discovered," he said at last, "that I don't like the idea of you stretching your fledgling wings in anyone's company but mine."

And before Cressida's protest reached her lips, Luke covered them with his.

ROBYN DONALD lives in northern New Zealand with her husband and children. They love the outdoors and particularly enjoy sailing and stargazing on warm nights. Robyn doesn't remember being taught to read, but rates reading as one of her greatest pleasures, if not a vice. She finds writing intensely rewarding and is continually surprised by the way her characters develop independent lives of their own.

Books by Robyn Donald

HARLEQUIN PRESENTS
649—AN OLD PASSION
665—THE GATES OF RANGITATAU
696—A DURABLE FIRE
904—AN UNBREAKABLE BOND
936—LONG JOURNEY BACK
952—CAPTIVES OF THE PAST
976—A WILLING SURRENDER
1040—COUNTRY OF THE HEART
1064—A LATE LOVING
1104—SMOKE IN THE WIND

HARLEQUIN ROMANCE
2391—BAY OF STARS
2437—ICEBERG

Don't miss any of our special offers. Write to us at the following address for information on our newest releases.

Harlequin Reader Service
901 Fuhrmann Blvd., P.O. Box 1397, Buffalo, NY 14240
Canadian address: P.O. Box 603,
Fort Erie, Ont. L2A 5X3

ROBYN DONALD

the sweetest trap

Harlequin Books

TORONTO • NEW YORK • LONDON
AMSTERDAM • PARIS • SYDNEY • HAMBURG
STOCKHOLM • ATHENS • TOKYO • MILAN

Harlequin Presents first edition December 1988
ISBN 0-373-11128-2

Original hardcover edition published in 1988
by Mills & Boon Limited

CHAPTER ONE

CRESSIDA GODWIN strove successfully to keep panic at bay. The bones which moulded her face showed stark beneath skin still gilded by a tropical sun as she drew in a deep, noiseless breath, straining to discern the voice through the static. Outside, the wind began to keen through the stays, harbinger of the storm which had been threatening for days.

'. . . to meet you,' the operator finished, the static fading momentarily so that the masculine voice sounded calmly, reasonably close. 'Do you copy, *Windhover?* Over.'

Cressida's teeth closed on her bottom lip, but her voice was just as calm. 'I copy you. Over and out.' Her hand shook with a combination of shock and weariness as she replaced the handset.

Without looking at the still form strapped to the bunk in the cabin below, she left the radio and went about the task of shortening sail, working efficiently and swiftly as the wind picked up strength, its whine lifting to a shriek.

Once, she lifted her head to look beyond the confines of the yacht towards a lee shore. That savage wind was pushing her towards a high, frightening line of cliffs where the waves would already be breaking ferociously in the swell that pounded in before the storm. Somewhere in that murk and spray was the entrance to the harbour, hidden, difficult to find in good weather, let alone bad. She knew this part of the

5

chart off by heart. Further south on the rugged
coastline of New Zealand was the wide, well-marked
entrance to the Bay of Islands, but she dared not wait
for that. The weather forecast had given her no cause
for confidence. Out there in the limitless reaches of
the Pacific Ocean a depression had turned vicious,
and she was directly in its path.

Cressida was not frightened, she could not allow
herself to be. It was hard work reefing the sails, but
she found freedom from the weight of her fears in
doing it with the methodical calmness her father had
inculcated in her over the years. When at last it was
done, she took the wheel and went about, heading
away from the coast, her slender black brows drawn
together as she waited for the sound of engines. Not
too far away the chart marked a small string of islands;
the northernmost appeared occasionally through the
spindrift, a threat she had to keep an eye on.

Only once during the next hour did her
concentration break, and that was when a small plane
flew overhead, clearly looking for her. Sudden, quick
tears stung the bright dark blue of her eyes; she had to
swallow hard to force down the lump in her throat. In
spite of appearances, she was not alone in this wild
waste of grey water beneath a sky which seemed to be
boiling with activity.

Not long after that, she caught her first glimpse of
the vessel which had come out to meet her. Cressida
knew the danger was not over, but she couldn't
prevent the surge of relief which flooded through her
body, bringing colour to her cheeks and a subtle
easing of the tension of the past day.

But she was once more rigidly controlled when the
deep roar of two huge engines broke through the howl
of the wind, presaging only by a few seconds the arrival

of the big deep-sea fishing launch.

What followed was a tribute to her father, who had taught her how to handle the yacht and to keep her head in an emergency, but even more to the man perched high above the ocean at the wheel of the other vessel, and his crew.

On the wheel, her hands stiffened with tension as the big boat eased quietly to windward, the huge engines keeping it far enough away for safety, close enough so that she could hear the man who shouted to her from the deck.

The wind snatched the words from his mouth, but she heard enough to make her wave and lift a jaunty thumb towards him.

Instantly, the fishing-boat dropped astern. The powerful engines snarled as it was positioned to leeward. Cressida groped in a locker, her teeth biting into a white lip as her fingers closed around tough cord. Straightening, she held the ladder high; the man on the deck of the other vessel gave her back her own gesture of understanding. Then he threw the coil of rope.

It missed, that first time. Cressida braced herself against the coaming, afraid against all reason that he would not make it. However, the second time it came straight and true, and she was ready for it, grabbing it before it had a chance to slither back, cleating it down twice before lifting her thumb again. Instantly, the big figure in the life-jacket, and very little else as far as she could see, went over the side of the big-game-fishing vessel.

Once more Cressida's teeth clamped down on her lip as she waited, the rope-ladder held in a death grip until the sleek dark head came up through the tossing waters. With powerful strokes he struck out for the slack rope.

She exhaled on a sharp release of tension as he grabbed it and came hand over hand towards the *Windhover;* as he came close, she realised with a kind of dull astonishment that his teeth were bared in a fierce, exultant grin. He looked like some pagan god of the sea, completely at home in the wild waste of water.

And then he was there, his great strength apparent in the ease with which he hauled himself over the coamings, climbing up the ladder as though he did this sort of thing all the time. Back at the wheel, Cressida watched from the corner of her eye as he released the lifeline. He raised a hand to the pilot of the launch before turning towards her, and she realised that she was looking at a giant of a man with the reckless laughter of a pirate in his eyes.

'OK?' he shouted into the maelstrom.

Unable to speak, she gulped and nodded.

'Right. I'll take over.'

With a sigh of relief she slipped back into her old role, that of underling. Somehow this unknown man inspired confidence, his big frame and the strong, clean-cut lines of his features radiating a masculine competence she was accustomed to, for her father had had it, too. It could hurt, that careless, arrogant confidence, and never know of the pain it inflicted, but it wouldn't let you down.

It took only a few wary minutes for her to accept that the man who had come in answer to her cry for help was as expert a sailor as her father; without appearing to, she watched as he drove the yacht through the wind into the rain which came cutting down almost immediately. He made use of the array of instruments at his command, but he seemed to rely as much on that certain inbuilt knowledge which comes of long experience on the sea. A safe distance away, the big launch kept watch over them, appearing and disappearing through the murk like a phantom vessel.

Cressida banned all thoughts of the Flying Dutchman, keeping her gaze fixed on the masterful hands of the man at the wheel. That alarming feral smile just touched the corners of a mouth at once hard and humorous; he had thrown off the bulky, clumsy life-jacket and stood in a thin black woollen jersey which clung like a sleek second skin to his big frame, revealing every contour beneath. He wore bathing shorts and, beneath them, long, heavily muscled legs shifted with the movements of the yacht, deeply tanned skin rippling over the corded strength of muscle and ligament.

After a while she went below and got him some of her father's clothes; they would be too small, but at the least the jersey would prevent hypothermia and the slicker would help keep him dry. He looked up as she touched his arm, saw what she had in her hands and nodded, handing over the wheel while he dried himself off with the towel she gave him and hauled the garments over his sleek dark head and massive shoulders.

She jumped as he said in her ear, 'Thank you,' but soon regained control of herself, giving him a thin smile as she relinquished the wheel.

Once, during a particularly vicious squall, Cressida's gaze darted without volition from her clenched fists up into the arresting symmetry of his face; she realised again that he was enjoying himself. He looked down at her; he must have seen the angry incredulity in her eyes, but his only response was that fierce, completely unabashed grin, making no attempt to hide his exhilaration. It was Cressida who looked away, wishing hollowly that she had that fine, Viking recklessness. It would make life much easier.

Hours later, after a hair-raising entrance into the harbour, with the storm driving at their heels, she worked with the ease of long experience at getting the sails down. Her father was—had been—a perfectionist, and she moved smoothly about the now almost stable decks of the yacht, stowing the sails and coiling ropes, until the man at the wheel said, 'Right, that's it. She's your boat, you take her in.'

She managed it, but her hands were trembling with reaction as she brought the yacht in against the wharf. After the turmoil out beyond the heads, it was almost serene in here, although it was still raining, and the high hills on either side of the narrow stretch of water gave birth to sudden, ferocious gusts which had to be watched, but there were no waves to speak of. And dealing with the gusts stopped her from worrying about the group of men who waited on the wharf.

But at last she could not push the thought of them away any longer. Held at bow and stern, the yacht was tethered to the land again, and with that came the realisation of her situation. She stood stupidly in her old slickers, her head bowed as two of the men swung on board.

From beside her, the man who had resuced her ordered tersely, 'Look at me.'

Startled, Cressida obeyed, lifting huge, unseeing eyes as dark a blue as the sky at dusk, and he said in a curiously toneless voice, 'I must be blind! You're a girl.'

'I was eighteen last birthday,' she told him politely, then looked past him to the policeman. 'I'm Cressida

Godwin,' she said.

As he shook hands, he surveyed her with considerable curiosity and some sympathy. After a moment he indicated the man behind him. 'This is Dr Gibbs.'

Nodding, she said in a chill little voice, 'How do you do? He's down below.'

With an impassive face, she watched the two men file down the companion into the cabin. A soft movement of the boat indicated that someone else had come on board. She paid no attention, waiting with all her attention fixed on what was happening below. The man beside her moved sharply past, said something to the newcomer. A different note in the hard, beautiful voice caught Cressida's attention; she turned and saw that he was preventing a man from coming aft to where she waited in the cockpit.

'Oh, come on, Luke, this is news,' the intruder half threatened, half pleaded, his eyes fixed avidly on Cressida. 'Give me a break!'

'I'll break your neck.' It could have been a genial comment, because the man called Luke smiled as he said the words, but there was no humour in his face or his voice. He suddenly looked a very tough customer indeed, and the reporter recognised it as clearly as Cressida, for he fell back and stepped on to the concrete of the wharf without any further attempts to speak to her. Luke whoever-he-was stood like a large menacing barrier, effectively blocking the way.

Not that anyone else seemed inclined to push their luck. There were more people on the wharf now; Cresida turned away, cutting herself off from the interested stares, the whispered comments. She looked out to the hidden entrance to the harbour, almost wishing herself back out there. At least then she hadn't had the opportunity to think.

The policeman stepped up into the cockpit, his tough, pleasant face frowning. 'I'm sorry about this,' he surprised her by saying. 'You're a New Zealander, aren't you?'

'Yes, although I haven't been here since I was eight, about ten years ago.'

'Got any relations here?'

She shook her head. Water was dripping down her back, so she pulled off the hood to reveal a black urchin crop, the wisps of fine hair plastered sleekly against her neat skull. 'Not that I know of. My mother has been dead for two years. I think all her family are dead, and my father never referred to any relatives.'

'Friends you can contact?'

She gave him a small, wry smile. 'We spent most of our life at sea. I don't know anyone here.'

From behind, the man called Luke said in a calm, totally assured tone, 'She can stay with me. After you've done with her, I'll take her home.' A note of irony crept into his voice. 'My mother is expecting her.'

Incredibly, the policeman seemed relieved. 'That would be an excellent idea,' he said heartily. 'We'd know where to contact you . . .'

He swung around as the doctor came up the companionway. In spite of the fact that she had known for over twenty-four hours that her father was dead, Cressida directed an imploring look at him. 'My dear,' he said compassionately, 'he died instantly. There was nothing you could have done to help him. Nothing.'

She nodded, blinking back unbidden, unwanted tears. By common consent, the men turned away, talking in low voices among themselves. Except for Luke. He didn't touch her, but she felt his gaze on her and lifted her chin to meet it. His eyes were pale, surprising in such a tanned face, the exact shade where green meets brown, shrewd and piercing, yet strangely kind.

'Keep it up for a little longer.'

That was all he said, yet somehow the few words of understanding gave her the courage to face the stress of the few hours that followed.

They were all very kind, but she was a problem for them, one they seemed only too glad to load on to Luke Scrivener's broad shoulders. Something in the way they did so revealed that they were accustomed to handing him responsibility of one sort or another.

Since the moment when she had gone to wake her father—was it yesterday morning or the day before that?—and found it impossible, she had been stretched to her limits; now, like the kindly busy men she had fallen among, she allowed Luke to take over, meekly accompanying him as he shepherded her on to the big launch when all the interviews were over.

'The *Windhover*—' she objected suddenly, stopping.

'It's all right, Stan's going to bring her down harbour to the station.'

An imperative hand on her shoulder urged her forward. It must have been exhaustion that made her think she could feel a current of electricity run from those long fingers right through her body. Pulling away a little, she concentrated on his next words.

'Stan was at the wheel of the launch, so you can trust him with your yacht.'

The deep-sea fishing rig was big and fast and luxurious, and Luke handled it as competently as the unknown Stan. Within a very short time they had crossed the harbour and were turning into a narrow,

rock-edged inlet with a sandy beach at the head of it.
To one side was a jetty backed by a large shed, almost
hidden beneath a canopy of branches. A quick glance
revealed that they all came from one tree, an
enormous sprawling thing with bold dark bark and
deep green leaves, silver-lined. Through the clamp of
shock, Cressida felt her heart lift a little. This then
was the pohutukawa her mother had missed so, the
toughest tree in New Zealand, happiest with its roots
and branches bathed in salt spray.

A large mooring accepted the launch. Although the
storm had increased in intensity so that the wind was
now shrieking down the harbour, the little cove was
snug and sheltered. A lifetime spent on the sea and in
a multitude of anchorages around the world gave
Cressida the experience to understand that very little
in the way of weather would bother anything moored
there. Numbly, she got into the dinghy, watching
with eyes which were dazed and cloudy as Luke
Scrivener unshipped the oars and bent his powerful
back to row the little craft ashore.

She made to help him carry the dinghy up the
beach, but he shook his head and, in a manoeuvre that
revealed his great strength, hoisted the thing up on to
his back and carried it into the shed.

Normally, Cressida would have been curious about
the interior of that shed, but she felt strangely
separated from her surroundings. She leaned on the
side and watched with a blank lack of interest as he
put the thing down and straightened up.

'How long is it since you had any sleep?' Luke
demanded as she hid a yawn behind long, sun-
darkened fingers.

'I don't know.' She calculated, forcing her brain to
work. 'Nearly thirty hours, I think.'

He said nothing, but picked up a bag she vaguely
recognised as hers, put a hand in the small of her back
and propelled her towards a large mud-streaked Land
Rover. The rain still held off; she stood quietly and let
him unfasten her wet-weather gear quickly and competently, as impersonally as if she were a child. He
even boosted her up into the front seat before
shrugging out of the slicker she had got for him and
flinging both garments into the back of the vehicle.

Cressida sat very still. He had hair the colour of a
wet chestnut and shoulders wide enough to fill the
sky. A big man, tall and broad and forceful, the kind
of man whose size was at once a threat and a reassur-
ance. His face was an indication of his character;
features carved from rock, tough and compelling,
promising a forcefulness that went beyond arrogance
to a calm, immovable strength.

A shudder, which was entirely unrelated to the chill
in her body, tightened her skin. Later she was to
realise that it was the first tingle of awareness.

As he turned the Land Rover inland over a well
graded metalled track Cressida's gaze fell to her
hands, suddenly tense in her lap. Never manicured
beyond the simplest filing, the fingernails were torn
and broken, on one, down to the quick, mute wit-
nesses to the ordeal she had just endured. Her eyes
slid sideways to the wheel. His hands were long-
fingered and tanned, the nails cut cleanly. Yet she had
felt calluses on them.

She looked away, slowly taking in the scenery
through the windscreen. Luke Scrivener was a farmer,
and worked hard on his land, but there was more to
him than that. He had an indefinable air of command,
a compound of the power of his personality and rock-
bound strength of will.

From somewhere deep inside Cressida felt another shiver rack her body.

'It's not far to go,' he said instantly.

She nodded and took a tight hold of herself, holding her body stiff in the seat.

After a few minutes he observed, 'We've had an exceptionally wet winter so far, but, as you'll see when we get to the house, it's now almost spring.'

'What sort of climate do you get here?' If she didn't talk he would think she was a half-wit, but her voice was husky with strain.

'Warm temperate. We can grow sub-tropical fruits, babacos, bananas in sheltered places, kiwi-fruit. About fifty inches of rain annually, with winter our wet season. Summer can be, and usually is, dry. Five Mile, which is the name of the station, is volcanic, as you can see by the rocks and the shapes of the hills.'

Sure enough, they were now climbing steeply between large, grey weathered boulders which thrust through the vivid grass, and the hills around the valley were carved into weird, surrealistic shapes with sudden precipices of purple-grey rock falling sheer from trees and grass. Absorbed, Cressida looked around, unaware that her expressive features revealed the interest replacing the apathy of a few moments ago. Unaware, too, of the small satisfied smile which pulled in the corners of his firm mouth.

Once over the brow of the hills, he told her laconically, 'You can see the homestead from here.'

It lay on a wide expanse of flattish land, high enough above the creek which had carved out this valley to avoid any flood; a big, rather Victorian building, painted white. In spite of the bleak day, the racing wind and low, scudding clouds, it seemed to lie in sunshine, surrounded as it was by gardens and wide lawns.

Cressida sighed, her face unguarded for a moment in an expression which was almost enraptured. Years ago, when she had been a solitary child, she had sometimes dreamed of a settled home, and always it had been something like this, a gracious structure old enough to be a part of its landscape with gardens and trees in a wide green valley. This was like a vision from her subconscious.

Belatedly, she became aware of the sharp lance of his eyes on her face. Something speculative in the crystalline amber depths made her hastily compose her features; instinct warned her that it would be dangerous to expose too much of herself to this man. In a neutral little voice she said, 'It's very lovely. How long have you lived here?'

'All my life.' He said it casually, as though people who spent all their life in one place were commonplace.

Cressida stifled a sigh, wondering if he knew how lucky he was. Probably not. Many people envied her and her father their gypsy life-style, because life in a yacht was romantic and exciting, but by the time she was thirteen she had had enough of excitement to last her a lifetime. All she wanted, all she longed for, with the fervour of a nomad seeking water in the desert, was a life spent in humdrum quietness.

As for romance . . . her father had written books romantic enough to turn the heart of the most confirmed sophisticate, but he had hidden that streak of romanticism with a brusquely practical facade he'd allowed no one, not even his daughter, behind.

Luke Scrivener seemed to understand her need for silence, for he said nothing more, leaving her unhappy thoughts to be cut short by the rattle of a cattlestop beneath the vehicle's wheels. Somewhere, a dog barked, and the note of the engine changed as the Land Rover pulled up on a wide paved court at the back of the house.

The storm might be doing its best to prolong the winter, but here it was spring. Pale sunlight picked out flowers against the house, sweet-scented freesias and daffodils and bright jonquils, the pink and white splendour of camellias, and a huge Taiwan cherry which presided in a cloud of cerise blossom over one side of the courtyard. Daphne flowers impregnated the cool damp air with their spicy, exquisite perfume, and by the back door a little low shrub flaunted tiny, crinkly crimson flowers against dark needles of foliage.

'Manuka,' Luke's crisp, deep voice told her. 'Also known as tea-tree because the first settlers used its leaves as a substitute for tea. A native of the country, although this particular one is a hybrid. Welcome to Five Mile, Cressida.'

Cressida didn't look at him, her whole attention held by the woman who came into the doorway. Tall and beautiful, with a merry, vital face, she was smiling, the light eyes she shared with her son sharp and perceptive.

'Yes, you're very welcome, my dear,' she said. 'Come on in, out of the cold.'

In later years, Cressida would say that one moment was all it took for her to learn to love Diane Scrivener, but all she was conscious of at that moment were the hot tears which stung her eyes and overwhelmed her in a choking, shaming flood. Gasping, she tried to stop them, knuckling at her eyes like a tired child. It was impossible. When Luke quickly and effortlessly picked her up, she turned her head into his chest and let the tears run as he carried her into the house.

His arms were hard and amazingly comforting; she heard his deep voice giving orders, counterpointed by his mother's, and then she was set down on a wide sofa in front of a fire and those arms held her head comfortingly against his chest. Cressida knew that she mustn't begin to cry again, that if she did she would lose control, but the tears kept on forcing their way through until in the end she surrendered and wept away the fear and tension.

What happened after that was a blur. Just occasional snatches fixed themselves in her brain, little cameos of recollection separated by long periods of sleep. There was the wonderful crispness of sheets against her skin, and the almost sensual pleasure of succumbing completely to the exhaustion which she had had to ignore for so long. Someone insisted on her drinking soup, and once, when she cried out in the night with a dream, she was held against a broad masculine shoulder and her back and hair stroked with a wonderfully comforting hand. And there was a cat, a large marmalade thing which was quite frequently removed from her feet.

When she awoke, she was alone and the sun was streaming across the beautiful rug which almost covered the wide polished boards of the floor. Cressida lay still for some time, her eyes roaming the room, surprised to discover that it was familiar to her. Somehow, during that long sleep, she had absorbed it into her brain, so that she recognised the watercolours on the wall and the tall secretaire with its glass doors and array of books. She even remembered the flowers, beautiful cymbidium orchids in soft subtle greens and pinks and golds, and daffoldils with the light of the sun imprisoned in their petals.

Most familiar of all was her hostess's face when she came quietly into the room.

'Hello,' she said softly. 'How are you feeling?'

'Embarrassed,' Cressida admitted shyly.

Mrs Scrivener chuckled. 'No need, my dear. You've been an exemplary patient. Phil Gibbs, the doctor, is very pleased with you.'

So she hadn't just dreamed the man's kindly face. 'What was the matter with me?' she asked.

'Exhaustion, mainly. You just needed to sleep.'

'I see.' Cressida sat up in the bed, startled at how reluctant her body was to obey her. 'How long have I been here?'

'Three days.'

'Oh, my goodness!' Appalled, she sagged back against the pillows. 'I'm sorry to be such a nuisance,' she said lamely.

'No nuisance, I promise you You did what you were told without protest, and in between you slept.' Her hostess's eyes, exactly the same as her son's, twinkled. 'A model patient!'

'I'm very good at doing what I'm told.' Now why had she said that? Cressida bit her lip and began again. 'What—what's happened? I mean—my father . . .'

'Luke has dealt with everything,' Mrs Scrivener told her gently.

Cressida shifted in the bed. 'That's very kind of him,' she said in a muted voice, uneasy, yet unable to discover the reason for such a reaction.

'Oh, Luke can be very kind. You know, I think you should have a shower if you feel up to it,' the older woman suggested. 'The bathroom is two doors down on the right. Can you walk that far?'

'I'm sure I can.'

But she was alarmingly unsteady on her feet, and

the short walk to the bathroom exhausted her. Cursing her weakness, she eased herself down on the chair, looking around her with appreciative eyes.

The bathroom was enormous, a compartmented affair panelled in a warm wood with an exquisite stained glass window taking up a large space on one wall. There were ferns in lush profusion and bright brass taps and an enormous bath standing proud on four clawed legs. It was warm and luxurious and totally different from any other bathroom Cressida had ever seen, at once at home with the period of the house and as modern as tomorrow.

She showered quickly, using a delicately scented soap, which someone had left out, on both her skin and her hair, before shutting off the water. Once more exhaustion clutched at her, draining her of energy. She had to sit down again before drying herself, and it was an effort to pull on a towelling wrap which hung on the wall. She ran a hand through her short damp locks, then, with her nightdress over her arm, went out through the door.

And coming towards her down the passage was Luke, tall and somehow daunting, in spite of the fact that he was smiling. It's those eyes, she thought apprehensively as she returned the smile. They seemed to be able to see into the centre of her soul, yet in spite of their clarity it was impossible to discern any emotion in their depths. They were strangely intimidating.

'Feeling more like yourself?' He had a voice like dark velvet, smooth and beautiful.

She nodded. 'Yes, thank you.' It cost her some effort, but she added, 'It's very kind of you to offer me hospitality.'

'I am,' he said, not quite hiding his amusement, 'a

very kind person.'

Cressida flushed, feeling gauche and stupid, and the teasing note in his voice was transformed into concern. 'I'm sorry,' he said unexpectedly and with immense charm. 'That was unfair of me. You're very welcome to stay here for as long as you want to. Both my mother and I enjoy having guests. All right?'

Cressida nodded, wondering dazedly if anyone ever said no to him. He had to know that when he smiled he was overpowering, a profoundly vital man with infinitely more than his share of attraction. Instinctively, she found herself comparing him to her father, and knew with a kind of bleak resignation that they were the same kind of man, possessed of a boundless magnetism, yet with a driving single-mindedness which could crush anything in the way.

'Your hair is wet,' he said, touching one of the black glossy locks on her nape.

A curious sensation thrilled through her. She stood very still, her eyes caught by his, every cell in her body aware of the almost imperceptible brush of his fingers against her skin.

'It dries quickly.' That was her voice, husky and impeded.

Something gleamed in his strange eyes until it was hidden by the secretive descent of dark lashes. He dropped his hand and stepped back. 'Hop back into bed,' he ordered, 'and I'll bring you a hairdryer. We can't have you catching a chill.'

She was able to breathe again, but her heart was still pounding when she got back to the bedroom, and for some silly reason she found it difficult to meet Mrs Scrivener's eyes. In her absence, the bed had been stripped and remade and a middle-aged woman was tidying up a vacuum cleaner. She exchanged smiles with Cressida as they were introduced to each other; she was the housekeeper, Mrs Collins.

Almost immediately she left, trailing the vacuum cleaner behind her, and Mrs Scrivener produced a nightgown. 'One of my daughter's,' she explained. 'She left it behind last time she was over from America. You and Sally are almost the same size, so it should fit.'

It was pretty, a floor-length affair of gold silky stuff, totally different from the cotton shirt that normally sufficed for Cressida. She felt awkward in it, but the knowledge that Luke could appear with the hairdryer any minute stopped her from delaying things by a protest. Hastily she scrambled into the frivolous little nothing, blushing at the almost total lack of concealment it afforded.

Sure enough, the knock on the door came before she was able to reach the sanctuary of the blankets, but he did not come in. Mrs Scrivener went across and took the dryer from him, came back and said, 'Sit up, my dear, and I'll do it for you.'

Which was just as well, for Cressida had never used one before. She sat patiently while the warm air played through her short black tresses, wondering about that unnerving little incident outside the bedroom.

It was, she supposed with a glibness gained from the magazines she had occasionally read, physical attraction. She could still feel the odd liquid sensation in the pit of her stomach, and the memory of that long, intense look tightened her skin into goose-flesh.

'Are you cold?' Mrs Scrivener switched off the dryer with a concerned look.

'Oh, no. No, I'm fine, thank you.' The stammering words brought a surprisingly sharp glance from the older woman.

'Then I'll bring you some breakfast. After that, Luke wants to talk to you.'

Unbidden, the sharp excitement of a few minutes ago sprang back into life. Cressida said something, she even smiled, but she had the uncomfortable feeling that she had not fooled Luke's mother; those eyes saw too much. However, Mrs Scrivener said nothing more before she left the room, and ten minutes later, when she reappeared with a pretty tray, there was nothing in her expression to make Cressida uneasy.

Breakfast was muesli with kiwi-fruit, toast and orange juice, and coffee.

'Eat it all up,' Mrs Scrivener ordered cheerfully as she set the tray on Cressida's lap. 'You could do with a little fattening.'

'I've always been thin.' But she was hungry, and she certainly felt much better when it was all gone, much more capable of dealing with the unsettling enigma which was her reaction to Luke Scrivener. Perhaps, she thought hopefully, it had just been hunger and weakness which had made her so absurdly sensitive to him.

Unfortunately for this theory, she felt exactly the same lurch of excitement when he walked into the room. He was so tall, and so big with it, wide-shouldered but with the narrow hips and long legs of an athlete. And he was, she realised in stunned astonishment, extraordinarily handsome, with an untamed male beauty which owed much to his striking bone structure.

Guiltily, she dragged her eyes away as he came on silent feet across to the bed, waiting with rapidly beating heart until he sat down in the chair he pulled up beside it.

'Feeling better?' he enquired, reaching out to tuck back a lock of hair.

Was it her imagination, or did his hand linger a fraction of a second in the hollow beneath her ear? A strange uncomfortable sensation, like a hot wire along her nerves, ran from her neck to her breasts.

With averted eyes she said hastily, 'Yes, thank you, much better. You—everyone has been very kind.'

'Good. Do you feel strong enough to talk about your father?'

Cressida nodded.

But he didn't begin straight away. Instead he asked, 'How long is it since you've been in New Zealand?'

'We—my mother and I—flew back when her father died, about ten years ago.'

'And since then you've been travelling?'

'Yes,' she said shortly.

'How did your parents organise your education?'

She shrugged. 'My mother taught me until I was high school age, then I went to a convent in England. My father had old-fashioned ideas about the right sort of education for adolescent girls.'

'You joined him straight from school?'

She bent her head, an old resentment hardening her oddly deep voice. 'After my mother died he needed a crew, so he took me away from school.'

'And did you enjoy the life?'

He wasn't worried about arousing her grief, that was for sure. 'Oh yes,' she said, masking the defiance in her tones with false enthusiasm. She was not going to have him pitying her. 'It was great fun.'

It was not entirely a lie. It had been fun, parts of it thrilling. Cressida had seen more wonders than most girls of her age; it was not her father's fault that she was a more conventional soul than he or her mother, that she hankered for stability and a settled home.

Luke said nothing, and she stole a look upwards to meet that clear, piercing, green-amber gaze. It was, she discovered, very difficult to lie to him. Colour burned into her cheeks and she hastily dropped her lashes, angry with herself for being so obvious.

'I see,' he said slowly. There was a pause which was tense and over-long, and she was glad when he said at last, 'The post-mortem revealed that your father died of a heart attack. It must have been instant. He woudn't have suffered.'

'I'm glad,' she said beneath her breath.

He nodded. 'I imagine he would have been glad to go like that, although he would have been horrified at the ordeal you suffered.'

Cressida, who thought she had a better understanding of her father's character, gave a cynical, hidden smile but said nothing.

After a moment he resumed, 'I remember that in one of his books he said that when he died he wanted to be buried at sea, so that's what I've organised. Is that all right?'

'Yes,' she whispered. Then, more strongly, 'He should be sent off like a Viking. That's what he would have liked.'

'Possibly, but I refuse to fire his ship about him. Besides, it's ferro-cement, isn't it? Difficult to burn.'

Perhaps he had expected open grief—that could have been the reason for the dry note in his deep tones. Cressida knew she was behaving strangely, but her emotions seemed to be frozen behind a mask. She didn't even know if she was sad that her father had died. Ever since he had insisted on her leaving school to join him in his eternal wanderings her main emotion towards him had been resentment. She had loved her time at school; the settled routine, the stability had been what she had longed for. She had been heartbroken when her father had taken her away. His cold refusal when she had told him she wanted to go on to university still made her angry and bitter. He had been a strange man, aloof, withdrawn, even with the wife he had loved dearly. When Cressida had been a child, she had been afraid of him.

Perhaps it was a carry-over of that childish fear which had kept her with him. That, and the fact that she had no skills, no education fit to get her a job. And no money. As long as she had done her job on the *Windhover* he had treated her with a remote friendliness which was probably the nearest he could get to affection. It was only when she suggested leaving him that he had become cruel.

She said now, wearily, 'I wanted to come ashore, but I didn't want it to happen this way.'

'That's life.' Luke sounded hard and unsympathetic, but when she looked up he was smiling, an oddly rueful twist of his lips as though he knew all about the bitter-sweetness of fate which gives while it takes away.

Unexpectedly, alarming her, he picked up her hand and held it firmly in his. 'At the risk of sounding pompous, it was no life for a girl of your age,' he said. 'You'd have been unnatural if you had enjoyed it. All those hormones surging around in your bloodstream looking for an outlet! Did he have to talk hard to drag you away from your boyfriends? He must have intended to drop you ashore fairly soon. Perhaps that's why he came back?'

She looked down at the hand enveloped by his, and wished it was soft and feminine, instead of sunburnt and callused with ugly, torn nails. Her pulses were leaping, beating so high in her throat that she thought she might not be able to talk around the thud of her heart.

'It don't know why he came back, he didn't confide in me. As for boyfriends, I told you he was pretty conventional. He had Victorian attitudes to that sort of thing.'

It was her voice that betrayed her, and she coloured furiously as a sardonic smile hardened his mouth. 'Poor Cressida,' he said ironically. 'No wonder you're harbouring a grudge!'

She removed her hand from his, her eyes suddenly as cold and cutting as blue quartz. 'He made sure there were few opportunities for dalliance,' she said with cool dignity. 'And none for consummation, if that's what you're trying to find out.'

Luke's mouth tightened. 'Yes, I suppose that was what I was trying to discover. Acquit me of impertinence, however. I was, in a roundabout way, trying to discover if you're at home in our liberated society.'

'Why?'

'Because, to a certain extent, that would dictate how we treat you.'

Cressida stared, her expression still frosty. He continued patiently, 'If you're a card-carrying member of the twentieth century, then we need have no qualms about throwing you out into the wide world. If, however, you're a pretty anachronism from Victorian days, then clearly someone is going to have to assume the status of a guardian until you succumb to the lure of present-day mores and morals.'

'I don't suppose you realise how patronising you sound!' she retorted indignantly.

The wide shoulders lifted in a slight, cynical shrug. 'It happens to be the truth.'

Cressida cast prudence to the winds. 'In that case, you'd better treat me as an anachronism. My father had strong views on women's place in the universe. Two paces behind the master when out, and in the kitchen at home.'

'Yet he treated you like a boy.' His keen gaze discomposed her. 'I've just read one of his books. It only slowly became apparent that the cabin boy was actually a girl.'

'He'd have preferred me to be a boy, certainly. At sea, it was easy enough to treat me like one.'

'And ashore?'

She frowned, her fingers quickly stilled from a sudden restlessness. 'He was very strict,' she said at last. 'He didn't like it if I made friends with—with anyone. He could be very intimidating.'

Luke lifted his brows at that, but gave her a sudden charming smile, at once taunting and understanding. 'So you were lonely,' he said.

She nodded. A silence enveloped them, warm yet shot through with tension. She made a deliberate effort to stop her fingers from their betraying movements, gazing sightlessly at their tanned slenderness against the white sheets.

After a moment he said without inflection, 'I think you'd better stay with us until you find your feet.'

'That's very kind of you,' she said slowly over the tears which were collecting in her throat, 'but you don't need to feel responsible for me.'

'I do. Have you any money?'

Her alarmed glance told him all he wanted to know. He said something succinct under his breath and went on, before it had time to register, 'Why don't you stay here until your father's affairs are organised? I can help you find a lawyer and anybody else you need, and you can entertain my mother. She enjoys house guests immensely.'

'I think you're the kind of person who has such broad shoulders that people are always dumping loads on them,' Cressida said shyly. 'I don't want to be a load.'

'I promise that as soon as you start to weigh me down I'll throw you out. Until then, you'll stay here.'

She laughed, because it was impossible to imagine anything he couldn't cope with, and said in a husky little voice which revealed a rather embarrassing relief, 'Yes, all right. Thank you.'

He smiled back at her, his striking features very controlled, but much to her relief said nothing more about it, and after a few teasing observations he left. When he had gone, she sat quite still, aware of a drumming excitement through her body which almost drowned out the suspicion that, in some way, she had exchanged one trap for another.

CHAPTER TWO

SURPRISINGLY enough, after the unconsciousness of the last two days, Cressida managed to sleep for most of that one too, waking only for meals.

But the next morning her eyes opened as the sun came up, and she lay for long moments perfectly still, looking down the length of her body. Last night Mrs Scrivener had gone to pull the curtains, but Cressida had asked her to leave them open. Now, entranced by the view from the window, she was glad she had made the request. To one side, the cherry tree flaunted its cerise blossoms, screening green paddocks where red cattle, slightly humped and Oriental-looking, grazed under a rich sky. The wind and rain she had dimly sensed through her dreams had blown itself out and the sun was shining on a wet, bright landscape, dramatic yet pastoral with those unusual cattle and the steep, strangely shaped hills which blocked out the rest of the world.

Cressida sighed, almost with relief. In an instinctive, atavistic way, she felt she had come home.

The room was warm; central heating, she thought as she pushed back the blankets and stood up. For a moment her head spun, but it steadied almost immediately. Bemused by the feel of the silky night-dress as it slid lovingly about her long legs, she walked across to the window.

Down below there was a wide stretch of lawn where thrushes and one large black-backed gull strutted. The grass curved past a huge jacaranda tree to a vine-hung wall which almost hid the dark green sparkle of a swimming pool. The gardens were big, surely far larger, she thought, than an ordinary farmhouse would have, and they bore the well-manicured air which denoted constant attention.

Luke Scrivener, she realised, was a very rich man.

Not that it mattered. She had promised to stay, but when all the formalities attendant on her father's death were dealt with she would have to leave Five Mile and find herself a place in this country which her mother had never stopped missing.

It was strange but, although she was a little concerned at being totally alone in the world, she was not frightened. She stood in the sunlight, which now poured in through the window, and felt its warmth on her skin and smiled, letting her eyes rest contentedly on that quiet green countryside.

In the middle distance, a man on a horse rode across a striated hillside, followed by two dogs. It did not need good sight to discern that it was Luke who bestrode the big piebald; he rode with careless ease, yet the set of his shoulders and the arrogant tilt of his head revealed his identity as clearly as if he wore a sign stating it.

Landscape with figures, Cressida thought, using flippancy to hide a slow, sweet melting in the pit of her stomach. Standing very still, she watched until the little group disappeared behind a clump of trees. They were heading towards the house, probably for breakfast, she decided. He must get up at an unearthly hour.

Sure enough, he was just coming in a side door as, clad in jeans and a jersey, she made her way hesitantly along a passage towards the scent of coffee.

She met his smiling greeting with a like response, unaware that her face revealed a hint of her powerful physical reaction to him. A flame turned the depths of his eyes from hazel to purest green. Cressida saw it and unwillingly felt it light little flares of response through her body.

Profoundly uncomfortable, she hurried into speech. 'I saw you on your horse, from the window.'

'Did you? Can you ride?'

'No.'

Luke said confidently, 'You'll enjoy it. I have a quiet gelding, ideal for a learner.'

A little spark of resentment impelled her to retort, 'I don't know that I want to learn, although it's very kind of you to offer to teach me.'

A raised eyebrow revealed what he thought of her ungracious answer, but he made no comment, merely saying, 'I'd better wash the smell of horse away. We eat breakfast in the morning-room, second door on the left. I'll see you there in a few minutes.

That lifted brow was enough to make Cressida feel crushed and gawky. As she turned away she bit her lip. It might be better if she waited to assert this new-found independence of hers until she left Five Mile; it was easy to see that Luke Scrivener was as little used to resistance as her father had been. His reaction to it was more subtle, but in its own way even more devastating.

In the morning-room, his mother was pouring herself coffee. Relieved to have something to take her mind off the encounter with Luke, Cressida exclaimed, 'Goodness, I'm hungry!'

'I'm sure you are, you haven't eaten much in the last three days. Those stunning cheekbones are dramatic enough for a model, but entirely too hollow for real life. Sit down and tell me what you'd like to eat.'

'I've always been thin.'

'Lucky girl!' Mrs Scrivener passed her a cup of coffee, chatting cheerfully in a fashion which required little in the way of answer, while she pressed food on to her guest until Cressida was sitting before a plate of bacon and eggs with a large glass of orange juice waiting for her attention.

She looked rather helplessly at it as her hostess told her that the oranges grew in the orchard, as did the kiwi-fruit in the bowl on the sideboard, and that the egg-shaped scarlet fruit with them were tamarillos.

'Absolutely my favourite fruit,' Mrs Scrivener confided, 'but they're an acquired taste. Sinfully delicious, stewed and served with cream or ice-cream. Or both. Ah, I was beginning to wonder if you'd decided to skip breakfast, Luke.' She beamed at him with an expression which said she was joking.

'Have I ever?' he asked in bland response as he sat down at the head of the table. He smiled affectionately at his mother, but although the smile did not fade when he looked towards Cressida it was not affection she discerned in his eyes. Instead there was that exciting lick of flame, quickly hidden behind hooded lids.

Uneasily, she looked down at her plate, surprised to find herself assailed by a ravenous hunger. She began the bacon and eggs with delicate greed, then demolished a piece of toast, listening rather desperately as mother and son talked, the elliptical, fragmented conversation of two people who could almost read each other's minds. She did not mind that they made little effort to include her; clearly, in this house, breakfast was a business meal during which the

Scriveners informed each other of developments and plans.

However, all too soon her attention was actively sought by Luke, who said, 'If you can come into the office after breakfast, Cressida, I'll give you your father's things. There's a sealed box which we found on *Windhover*. Presumably it has all the necessary papers in it.'

Her sense of wellbeing subsided into a faint nausea. Nodding stiffly, she finished her coffee, wondering if they regarded her as an unnatural daughter because she showed so little emotion over the death of her father. If so, the person to be blamed, she decided with a spurt of uneasy defiance, was her father. She hadn't wanted him to die, she just no longer wanted to be with him. All her life she had tried to love him, but his frigid lack of response had withered her childish, innocent expectation of affection.

The office was a big, book-panelled room, as Victorian as the rest of the house, so the computer set-up she glimpsed in an alcove looked shatteringly out of place. Luke must have noticed that swift glance, for he said easily, 'With the situation the way it is, farmers need every help they can get.'

'Are things very bad?' she asked, to put off the moment when she would have to approach his desk where her father's box sat.

Broad shoulders lifted. 'About as bad as they've ever been. Established farmers can weather almost anything unless the overseas market collapses completely, which is highly unlikely, but young men starting out and the hill-country farmers who rely heavily on fertiliser for continued production are finding it hard to keep their heads above water.'

'I know so little about New Zealand,' she said

quietly, 'but the recession has been almost worldwide, hasn't it?'

'Yes, and we're better off than many. In a way it's been good for us, jolted us out of complacency, but things have been extremely hard for those out of work.'

Helplessly, her eyes followed his lean-hipped stride across to the desk and she found herself wondering how tall he was, what he looked like beneath the fine material of his shirt. About six foot two or three, she thought, and from the ease with which he moved and the outline of his torso beneath the shirt he would be all muscle, hard and exciting. Unbidden, there floated into her mind a memory from the day they had met. She could see him at the wheel, the dark fine wool of his jersey plastered to that torso, revealing every rippling movement, and the strong columns of his legs . . . From nowhere came a wicked little image of all that strength and power bent to subduing a woman in the most primitive battle of all, that of the sexes.

Such speculations had never bothered her before. Disturbed and angry with herself, she grabbed for her usual reserve as he indicated the box.

'There it is. The firm of lawyers who dealt with your father's affairs contacted me as soon as your name made the papers. Fortunately, I know one of the partners and he's on his way up now, he should be here any minute. It almost certainly isn't necessary for him to be here when you open the box, but bear with me. I'm a cautious man.'

Cressida could have laughed at that. He looked the most unlikely candidate for caution she had ever seen. The striking contours of his face expressed nothing so much as a superb recklessness, although the hard lines of his mouth and the jut of his chin hinted at a self-control as strong as the boldness.

An unaccustomed dryness in Cressida's throat and mouth obstructed speech. Dazzled by sensations which seemed to clog her thought processes, she dragged her reluctant eyes away, welcoming the housekeeper's knock on the door with a fervour out of all proportion to its importance. Mrs Collins ushered in the lawyer, who was about the same age as Luke but stood an inch or so shorter, with shrewd grey eyes and a pleasant, rugged face. He was called Sam Thorburn.

Cressida took a deep breath, struggling for a degree of composure while Luke introduced them. After greeting her, the lawyer said quietly, 'I have with me a copy of the will your father left with us when he was last in the country, on the occasion of your mother's death. You were then still at school, I believe. I imagine that another copy is in this container. Are you quite happy to have me act for you in this matter, Miss Godwin?'

'Yes, except that I don't know if I can pay you. I haven't any money.'

Luke said curtly, 'That's the least of your worries, but, as Sam will explain to you, any expenses will be a charge on your father's estate, not on you. Do you want me to open the box?'

She nodded, aware of the way the lawyer's eyes moved from her to Luke and back again. She couldn't see any expression in them; in his own way he was just as poker-faced as Luke, and she wished suddenly that she was somewhere a long way from here. Everything had suddenly become very complicated.

From beneath her lashes, she watched as Luke quickly and brutally unsealed the metal container, his long fingers dealing deftly with the locks and seals.

Inside were papers, a whole bundle of them, and a photograph. When Luke held it out to Cressida, tears burned like acid in her eyes. 'My mother,' she said harshly.

He came around the desk to hold her against him for a moment, his arm around her shoulders. He smelt of warm male and his shoulder was very hard and comforting beneath her cheek. She heard the rumble of his voice and lifted her head, embarrassed, to meet the lawyer's eyes, sharp with a quickly banished emotion.

'All right?' Luke asked, turning her so that he could see her face.

She nodded as she stepped away, touching her handkerchief to her stinging eyes, using it as a shield so that he couldn't see how violently that impersonal offer of comfort had affected her.

'Yes, there's a copy of the same will here,' Sam Thorburn told them, looking back at the papers in his hands. 'Beyond that, there's not much else—passports, copies of various birth certificates, everything that's needed to prove identification. Do you want me to explain the will to you?'

As Cressida nodded, Luke said, 'I'll leave you to it. Call me if you need me.'

Feeling as if her one stay in a rocky world had left her, Cressida invited the lawyer to sit down. It would be horribly easy to become dependent on Luke's strength, she thought warily as she sat in the chair held for her. Far too easy.

She forced herself to attend closely to the lawyer's crisp voice explaining the terms of her father's will. They were simple enough. He had left her everything in trust until she was twenty-five.

'I have very little idea of the size of his estate,' Sam

Thorburn told her, watching her with a keenness which was not offensive. 'That will all have to be cleared up before we can apply for probate. I'll contact his publishers and his agent, and there is correspondence here from a man who appears to be his business manager. He could well have the complete picture. Do you have any knowledge of his affairs?'

Cressida shook her head, feeling totally inadequate. 'No, my father didn't discuss money with me. There never seemed to be any shortage, though.' She looked down at her hands. He had never discussed anything with her. Hers not to reason why . . .

She gave a funny little grimace and lifted her head to find the lawyer's uncomfortably perceptive glance on her. Quickly she said, 'I think his books sell well. He always seemed quite pleased with the royalties. He didn't seem to worry about money. He always bought exactly what he wanted for the boat . . .'

He nodded, looking away to tidy the papers into a neat pile. 'Luke told me that you've accepted his mother's invitation to stay here until we've cleared up this matter. I think that's very sensible of you. I can arrange to advance you a sum of money which will cover your immediate needs.'

He named an amount which lifted Cressida's eyebrows almost to the soft sable wisps of hair over her forehead, but as she had no idea of prices in New Zealand she said nothing.

'May I give you some advice?'

Startled, she looked up. 'Yes,' she said cautiously.

He grinned. 'It's an occupational hazard when you're dealing with lawyers. We're trained to advise people. In this case, it's very simple. You're probably still in shock, so try not to make any decisions now.

Just coast along. Mrs Scrivener is noted for her love of company, she'll enjoy having you here immensely; let her show you the way around. Life on these big stations can be very pleasant, especially in summer, and that's not too far away now. In a way, it's like a slice of life from the past. Many places like this are now owned by family trusts and run by managers, but Luke owns Five Mile outright. The Scriveners are one of our big pastoral families, with properties all down the country, and Luke grew up knowing that it would all be his responsibility. It's had quite an effect on his character. He's a hard man and he can be arrogant, but he's totally trustworthy. Treat your stay here as a holiday, a period of rest and recuperation.'

She smiled faintly. 'Do I look as though I need it?'

'You're altogether too fine-drawn about the eyes and temples and mouth to look the picture of health. To put it bluntly, you're under stress, and it will take time for you to deal with it.' He paused, so that she looked up, and then he resumed deliberately, 'You will, of course, fall a little in love with Luke. You can trust him not to take advantage of that. His reputation with women is not spotless, he's an attractive man and has been much pursued. He wouldn't be human if he hadn't taken advantage of his opportunities, but he knows the rules. You'll be quite safe with him.'

Cressida's blush was fiery, the colour burning through the clear olive of her skin in a way that embarrassed and humiliated her. In a gruff little voice she said, 'Thank you for your advice.'

'You don't mean that now, I know,' he said gently, 'but you will in time. You have a "little girl lost" air which is amazingly appealing, and Luke is no more immune to it than I am. I gather you've been cloistered by your father, no doubt with the best intentions, but from now on your life will be very different and you'll have to learn to take care of yourself. I'm sorry if I've offended you.'

She shook her head. 'You haven't. I know you mean well. I'll try not to make too big a fool of myself.' A thought struck her. She slid a swift look at him through her lashes and said, 'Perhaps I could fall a little in love with you. That would be safer, wouldn't it, as you're a long way away in Auckland?'

There was a moment's silence, and Cressida thought she had really put her foot in it, but after a moment he began to laugh softly, and suddenly she realised that he was an extremely attractive man.

'My mistake,' he said as he got to his feet. 'I should know better than to offer gratuitous advice, even to a girl who looks as though nothing of the world has touched her. By all means, fall in love with me, Cressida, I should be honoured. I can think of nothing more exciting than to have two beautiful women in love with me. My wife assures me that even after three years of marriage she still feels the same.'

He was nice, she liked him very much, and her eyes said so, twinkling up at him as she too got up. Still laughing, he took her by the elbow and escorted her from the room.

Luke was coming towards them, treading as lithely and softly as a cat along the passage. Cressida looked way up into eyes suddenly cold and clear as quartz; her smile died and she pulled herself free from Sam's grip. For one ridiculous moment, she felt a chill of anger emanate from the man who stopped in front of them. Then it was gone, and she was left bewildered and a little frightened, because for that moment she had felt as she used to feel when her father was angry with her—sick and powerless and afraid.

But Luke was not her father, he had no authority over her. Her chin rose; she looked directly at him, daring him to say anything.

He ignored her spurt of defiance, smiling lazily as he said in a voice which was coloured with nothing more than pleasant interest, 'All over? Come and have a drink, Sam, and flirt with my mother. She's expecting you to stay the night, by the way. You should have realised that and brought Angie with you.'

Sam grinned, informing him with a pride he made no attempt to hide, 'Can't be done, she's pregnant and travelling makes her feel sick.'

This was cause for celebration. Mrs Scrivener was delighted, agreeing without demur that of course Sam would have to go straight back, and asking numerous questions about Angie, who was clearly a favourite. Cressida sat and listened, her eyes travelling from one to the other but avoiding Luke. Sam Thorburn had been ridiculous to suggest that she might fall in love with him; she didn't know the man, and what little she suspected about his character frightened her! So, although he looked and moved with all the dangerous attraction of the forbidden, secure and totally self-assured, he was quite safe from the embar-rassment of becoming the object of any crush.

And if will-power didn't work, at least she could make sure that he didn't know about her feelings. It was, after all, quite acceptable for a woman to feel a little hero-worship for a man who had come to her out of a wilderness of terror and storm and brought her into a safe harbour.

She smiled, her generous mouth a little ironic, and at that moment Luke looked over and caught her eye. He said nothing, merely lifted a dark brow, but within five minutes the lawyer was out in the Land Rover and Cressida and Mrs Scrivener were waving goodbye as it shot off across the paved yard.

'Where's Luke taking him?' asked Cressida.

Mrs Scrivener smiled. 'Out to the airstrip. He came up from Auckland by plane—it's so much quicker than driving all that way. Now, what would you like to do today? How are you feeling? You look a little weary; do you think perhaps you should have a rest before lunch?'

'No, oh no, I'm not tired!' Her protests died under the older woman's sapient regard and she smiled. 'Well, just a little. I don't know why, though. Normally I'm full of energy.'

'Shock,' her hostess told her concisely. 'The doctor told us to watch you for a week or so. Did Luke tell you that the coroner's inquest is tomorrow? You'll have to give evidence, but it shouldn't be too much of an ordeal. Luke will help you through it. And he's organised a memorial service for your father the day after tomorrow. It will be a very small one in the church, and after it we'll take his ashes out through the heads and scatter them at sea. Is that what you wanted?'

'It doesn't seem as though I have much choice,' muttered Cressida, then, blushing fervently, hurried on, 'I'm sorry, yes, that will be fine. But is L—— is your son always so bossy?'

'Yes,' his mother said firmly, the green-brown eyes, so like her son's suppressing a twinkle with difficulty. 'But the really irritating, topmost infuriating thing about him is that he's always right! When I'm absolutely seething about his calm assumption of authority he says, so politely that I could hit him, "Well then, what do you think should be done?" And I realise that

I have nothing better to offer. I've never been able to fault him yet! It's terribly annoying!'

Such teasing indulgence was new and unfamiliar to Cressida. She didn't quite hide the astonishment in her eyes as she looked at Luke's mother, and she wondered why the older woman's expression softened into compassion.

Mrs Scrivener frowned before saying briskly, 'Come and tell me what you think of our disposal of the things from the yacht. As soon as the storm died down, Luke organised the removal of almost everything from her, which we've stored in one of the storerooms. I'll show you where they are.'

That night, after dinner, Luke looked up from his newspaper and caught Cressida in the middle of a prodigious yawn. He grinned, then got up and came across to where she sat in a large armchair and held out a hand to her. 'I want to speak to you before you go to bed. Come along to the office.'

Cressida couldn't prevent the harried glance she directed at his mother, but she allowed herself to be half lifted out of the chair and urged across the room. 'Say goodnight to Mother,' he ordered in his blandest voice.

She stared indignantly at him, but lowered her lashes at the gleam in his eyes. 'Goodnight, Mrs Scrivener,' she said stiffly.

'Goodnight, dear. Sleep well.'

He took her hand and led her along the passage, totally ignoring her attempts to free herself. Once there, he seated her before leaning back against the desk to look down his angular beak of a nose at her and saying, still in that suspiciously smooth voice, 'I believe you need some clothes.'

Her lips tightened. 'Not really, and anyway, I can't

buy any until the advance that Mr Thorburn promised me comes through.'

She sensed rather than saw the lifted eyebrow. 'Sam? Ah, yes. Did you like him better than you do me? He's devoted to his wife.'

'I gathered that,' she said, goaded into anger and blushing furiously.

'Say my name.'

Totally bewildered by the soft command, Cressida stared at him. His sculptured mouth was curved into a smiling line, but the tanned skin stretched tight over features which were hard as stone and all masculine authority. Cressida went very still. She could hear the clock ticking quietly from the hall; as the silence stretched, the mellow sound of the chimes floated sweetly through the door.

She swallowed and said, 'Luke.'

And he laughed deep in his throat and said, 'It sounds good in that husky little voice.'

He was watching her openly, the sudden intensity of his gaze stirring her pulse points into unwonted activity. She felt his eyes as though they were touching her with fire, smoothing and stroking in swirls of flame over her body. And she thought dazedly of the lawyer's assertion that Luke knew the rules—whatever the rules were, because if this was the way he went about treating every woman he had in his house, no wonder they thought they fell in love with him!

'Now, about these clothes,' he said just before the tension forced her to her feet. 'You must realise that you'll need more here than you would on board your father's yacht.'

She nodded reluctantly, using the movement to lower her face so that he couldn't see her so clearly.

'So I'll advance you a sum of money. Mother will take you down to Whangarei to buy a few things which should see you over until the lawyers send you an advance.'

It made sense, of course it did. Cressida began to see why he irritated his mother so! A fall of blue-black hair slid across her heated cheek as she nodded again.

'All right.' Her voice was small. She hated the effect he had on her, and it hurt in an obscure way for him to lend her money.

All her life she had been dependent on her father, forced to ask for money to buy anything, and made to account for it. It had always humiliated her. Now it seemed as though that humiliation would never cease.

'I'll take you into the bank and organise it,' Luke told her, and then, in an unexpectedly kind voice, 'You look bushed, you sad little scrap. Do you want something to help you sleep?'

This time Cressida shook her head. She sought for the power to answer him, but her voice wouldn't obey her, and to her horror she felt sobs thicken in her chest.

It seemed that she had always needed the solid support of his arms and his shoulder, the almost tender comfort of his silence and presence. She wept her heart out, and when she recovered found herself curled up in his lap, cuddled against him in an embrace which held a marvellous consolation.

'Feel better?' asked Luke gently.

'Yes. I'm sorry . . . I'm sorry, I seem to spend all of my time bawling all over you!'

His hands pressed on either side of her face, tilting it so that he could see it. He was smiling, but without humour. 'My dear, crying is a necessary part of grief. Don't try to keep it in. You need to do it.'

But Cressida bit her lip and struggled free of him, smoothing down the length of her one good dress with fingers that trembled. He would think she was unnatural if she told him that she was not crying so much for her father as for herself. She could not imagine that her father was anything but happy, joined now with the woman he had loved, or in complete oblivion. He had never given Cressida any indication that he felt anything for his daughter but a remote sense of responsibility.

Shivering, because she recalled the long, silent days with him only too vividly, she said in a choked voice, 'Thank you. You're very kind. I think I want to go to bed now.'

The inquest was short and to the point. The doctor who had performed the post-mortem gave evidence of a massive heart attack; the coroner was fatherly and helped Cressida through her evidence. She knew that she was pale and tightly wound up, but her voice was steady, almost emotionless. Everyone ignored the reporters, and afterwards she was whisked away in a big BMW by a protective Luke. Back at the homestead, Mrs Scrivener suggested that Cressida rest.

'No, put on some jeans and you can come out with me,' Luke said autocratically.

Cressida didn't even demur. She felt strangely empty, and when she looked at herself in the mirror the blue depths of her eyes were flat and opaque, her mouth held in such firm control that it was thin and straight. As she zipped up her jeans, she noted absently that she had lost quite a lot of weight in the past few days. Both the shirt of deep rose-pink brushed cotton and the jersey she pulled on over it hung loosely on her slender frame.

Downstairs, she said in a subdued voice, 'I haven't any boots.'

Luke's brows lifted as he regarded her narrow feet. 'We probably have a spare pair of gumboots. They'll do for now.'

She nodded, pulling them on in the room that held rain gear and umbrellas and the other odds and ends so necessary on a farm.

Once outside, some of her lethargy fell away, driven from her by enjoyment in the crisp blue day. Although spring had definitely arrived, the breeze had a chilly nip, and she huddled into her yellow slicker with a keen appreciation of its resistance to the cutting edge of the wind.

The Land Rover was heavily mud-spattered, its entire back seemingly filled with large, vociferous dogs. However, at Luke's snapped order they stopped barking instantly and resolved themselves into two, black and white and lean, with sharp, intelligent faces.

Cressida eyed them dubiously. She was not particularly accustomed to animals of any sort, and teeth seemed to figure largely in their countenances. Luke said casually, 'The one with the tan patch on its flank is Jack, the other's Shep. Hold your hand out, palm down, and let them smell you. They won't bite unless they think you're going to steal a sheep.'

Tails wagged at the sound of their names. Slowly Cressida insinuated her hand towards the closest dog, surprised at the delicacy with which they familiarised themselves with her scent. 'Now what?' she asked.

'Now they know you. You can stroke between their ears if you want to.'

She did, and both dogs seemed to like it. Cressida did, too. She said their names, and was rewarded with writhings and open appreciation and much tail-wagging, even a lick on her hand. Her face lit up; she turned astonished eyes up to the man who watched, half smiling, and said on a laugh, 'I don't think I've ever stroked a dog before!'

A muscle pulled in his cheek. He looked suddenly saturnine. 'No? Well, I suppose there's not much space on a yacht for any animal.'

'Lots of people have cats,' she said, turning away so that he couldn't see the sudden dimming of her expression.

'But not you.'

'No, my father said animals were a nuisance, and that it wasn't fair to coop them up on board.'

Not for anything would she let him know how she had yearned for a pet. She did not want him to feel sorry for her.

'Fair enough, I suppose.' Luke stretched out a long arm to open the door, and she scrambled in.

Once inside and moving, she asked, 'Where are we going?'

'Across to check out a trough and look at some lambs.'

'New ones?'

'Not that new. We lamb up here in the autumn,' he said, his cheeks creasing into a smile. 'Our winters are warm enough, and as we have long dry summers it's best to get them well grown before the drought hits. Volcanic land like this dries out badly.'

She nodded, looking around her with interest. 'It looks very fertile,' she volunteered.

'Basically it is, but the soil has little humus and our high rainfall leaches it badly. The minerals drain down to the sea.'

Ahead, a watercourse wound its way down from the hills. Cressida followed its course with her eyes and asked, 'Is that why you've left all the trees around the streams?'

'One of the reasons. Fertiliser washed into the creeks is a major pollutant. The best way to keep it where it belongs is by retaining the trees. Also, they help prevent erosion, and they provide a suitable environment for birds. New Zealand has some of the rarest birds in the world, all in danger of extinction. We don't have a very good record, starting with the extinction of all the moa species through over-hunting and then the careless mowing down of species after irreplacable species.'

It was clearly a subject dear to his heart. Fascinated, Cressida listened as he told her of one of the success stories, the Chatham Island robin, a tiny black bird which was saved through the loving care of the Wild Life Department and the fecundity of a female bird nicknamed Old Blue, who was the parent of most of the twenty-two birds left.

'She's dead now,' he said as he swung the vehicle off a gravelled farm road to a narrower track which immediately began to climb. 'But through her efforts the robin is a little less likely to become extinct.'

Cressida nodded soberly, recalling the small dots of the Chatham Islands on the chart, eight hundred miles to the east of the main islands of New Zealand in the vast empty expanses of the Pacific Ocean. Her eyes swept over the vivid green pastures and up to the steep grey scarps which formed the castellated hills around the valley where the homestead lay.

'Life must have been very exciting around here when those cliffs were being formed,' she observed. 'They remind me of Tahiti, only these seem a little less jagged.'

'That's because they're older. What you can see are

the solidified lava plugs of ancient volcanoes. The ash and scoria ejected by the vents has eroded down into soil in the valleys, but these are going to take a while to do that.'

Luke told her their names, euphonious Maori words, and insisted she pronounce them properly, saying after her first stumbling attempts, 'After all, you are a New Zealander, even if you've never lived here.'

'Is this still an active volcanic field?'

'Not here. Down in the Bay of Islands, where you'll be able to see volcanoes almost in their pristine state, the last actual eruption was less than two thousand years ago, which geologically speaking is no time at all. They could have an eruption any time. But it's not likely up here.'

He stopped the vehicle at a gate, slanting a teasing smile down at her. 'First rule on any farm—the passenger opens and closes the gates.'

Laughter brightened her eyes to the clearest, brightest blue, the colour of the sky at twilight. 'That sounds eminently reasonable.'

But he got out to show her how to manage the big heavy thing, and waited while she stood and gazed about them, bemused by the loveliness. They were high enough to be able to see over the intervening hills to the coast and the wide sweep of the sea, darkly blue and still turbulent. The islands Cressida had been so wary of in that frightening last leg of the voyage lay like a handful of currants scattered across a bench.

She shivered and turned to the land, her profile pure and unclouded as she took in the sweep of hills, some as green as the one she stood on. Others, more distant, were blue and mysterious with a dense cover of forest. The country had a spare, quiet air, dramatic and aloof, the smooth contours of the farmland opposed to the stark abruptness of the crags that towered above it.

'That hill down there is terraced,' she observed, pointing. 'Not like the sheep tracks, though. Is the terracing artificial?'

Luke nodded. 'A *pa*.' At her enquiring glance he elaborated, 'The Maori normally lived in small villages, but when threatened they retired to fighting *pa*, forts built on steepsided hills, or cliffs.' His arm came about her shoulder, turning her, and he pointed out towards the coast again. 'See, to the left of that freighter, there's one there. It stands on a three-hundred-foot-high cliff, and until the arrival of fire-arms was impregnable. The terraces were protected by great palisades of tree-trunks.'

His arm was heavy and far too disturbing, yet Cressida couldn't move. Her stomach lurched, then seemed to drop. If this was how a crush was going to affect her, it was so alarming she would much rather not develop one!

Very firmly, she fixed her eyes on to the crag on the coast and muttered some sort of reply. It seemed an age until he said calmly, 'We'd better move on, I suppose.'

So, obviously, her nearness didn't have the same effect on him! Telling herself very sternly that she was being utterly stupid, Cressida followed him back into the Land Rover and occupied herself all the way down the hill by staring with great determination out of the window.

They passed some of the vivid cattle, red as the volcanic soil which gave them sustenance, and she admired their deerlike heads and the great sleepy eyes.

'They're Santa Gertrudis,' Luke told her. 'Mostly Shorthorn with some Brahmin. They like the heat and they don't get ticks.'

She nodded, then exclaimed as they rounded a hill and a flock of goats rushed up to the fence. 'Aren't they sweet! What sort are they? I love those horns.'

He grinned. 'Angora. They're shorn for their fibre.'

Cressida said in a puzzled voice, 'Surely this is a mixed farm? I thought most New Zealand farms just had one sort of animal on them.'

Luke stopped and got out, striding around the front of the vehicle to open her door. 'It used to be that way, but the economic situation has forced us to diversify. Come on, you can take a closer look at them. They're stud animals, spoilt abominably by the studmaster's family.'

The goats were charming, with alert, mischievous faces which reminded her of a photograph of a white Persian kitten she had saved from a magazine many years before. As one nibbled interestedly at her fingers she remarked on it, unaware that for a moment her face was shadowed by her childhood longing for a pet.

'Did you want a Persian kitten?' he asked, and she shook her head, turning her face away to present him with her composed profile.

'Any kitten would have done.' She smiled, dismissing the matter. 'What else have you on this farm of yours?'

'Deer.'

The laconic reply surprised Cressida into looking up at him. His face was quite expressionless, except for two grooves in the skin on each side of his mouth. A cold chill feathered across her skin. He looked—angry, with a deadly cold anger unlike anything she had ever encountered before. Inwardly shrinking, she followed him back to the Land Rover and waited until the silence threatened to become too unnerving before asking him where the deer were kept.

'As far away from the road as possible,' he said a little grimly, and when she turned him a startled face he nodded. 'We have rustlers here, too. We haven't lost anything, but further south there have been a lot of incidents.'

The idea of stock-rustling seemed so far removed from the idyllic surroundings that Cressida couldn't believe it. It must have shown in the blue clarity of her eyes, for he began to tell her of events which astounded her, of great trucks driven through cut fences and whole herds of goats and deer rounded up and spirited away, deer airlifted by helicopter from paddocks in the dead of night, farm tractors and machinery removed when the owner had gone out for the day.

'Out security is pretty tight,' he finished, 'but nowadays in one-man operations theft can be the difference between going under and staying solvent.'

'Have you never lost anything?'

She didn't know why she asked, and his response made her sit back in the seat, wishing she hadn't. Luke's face hardened and he said briefly, 'Yes. Someone thought that the launch would make a good method of getting from here to Whangarei.'

'What happened?'

His jaw tightened. He looked suddenly brutal and very very dangerous. 'I went out in the helicopter and found them.'

Cressida drew a deep breath. The forbidding tone of his voice warned her against probing further but, that night, when he was busy in his office and she was sitting with Mrs Scrivener, she mentioned it.

His mother looked up from the crossword she was doing and gave her a long, considering look. 'It wasn't particularly pleasant,' she said at last. 'They were a couple of kids, about seventeen. Luke, of course, had no idea how old they were and was absolutely furious. He took the chopper out and forced them back into the harbour in a display of flying that terrified the life out of them. Just hearing about it makes me so glad I wasn't there! When they came back inside the heads, they were intercepted by Sam and a couple of the men from the station and the policeman, and Sam told me they were in tears. Luke had flown so close to them that they thought he was going to hit them. Dangerous, of course, but Luke can handle the chopper as if it were a sewing machine, and he has a streak of rashness a mile wide. Most of the time it's well under control, but when he lets it loose—look out!'

Cressida nodded, thinking of the contradiction between the bold lines of his face and that austere mouth. Yes, she could imagine how terrifying he must be in a temper. 'What happened to the thieves?' she asked diffidently.

Mrs Scrivener smiled. 'They went before the courts, and were put on probation. Luke arranged for them to be put to work on the farm. That was three years ago, and they're still here.'

Still more contradictions. Cressida bent her head over her book, but the print danced before her eyes, and between them and the page she could see her host's face, and wonder at the character of a man who would behave like that.

When she looked up again, Luke was coming in through the door, leanly elegant in a silk shirt and narrow trousers that hugged his hips and powerful thighs. The light from the small chandelier gleamed golden and bronze and chestnut in his thick hair. A strange melting sensation slithered through her body. Nervously, she bit her lip.

'Finished?'

He nodded at his mother's query, then fixed Cressida with an amused glance. 'Can you drive?'

Warily, she shook her head. 'There's not much call for that skill at sea,' she said.

His brows drew together. 'There's plenty of need for it on land, however. You'd better learn before you leave us. Mama, may we use your car? No, it's an automatic, isn't it? We'll use the BMW. One should learn to drive in a car with gears.'

Cressida said with considerable emphasis, 'I can't take up anybody's time——'

'My time,' he said crisply, 'and I'm quite sure it won't take long.'

'Yes, but——'

'Just agree,' his mother advised, smiling. 'Otherwise you'll find yourself still protesting as you sit for your licence.'

Cressida sat mutinously, her mouth constricting into a stubborn line. She, who had never openly opposed her father, was damned if she was going to let Luke Scrivener take his place and order her about! The light of battle flamed in her eyes as she looked up, and met an amused and sympathetic smile which suddenly cut the ground from beneath her feet.

'You must learn to drive,' he said, laughter not far away, adding with a low cunning which revealed how well he read her, 'Otherwise you'll be dependent on others to ferry you about.'

She returned acidly, 'You might have asked, instead

of telling me!'

He did laugh then, and came over to sit beside her. 'Blame it on my autocratic father,' he said. 'He once told me that it saves a lot of time if you just inform instead of asking. The years have convinced me that he was quite right.'

Reluctantly, because he was using his charm quite without shame, Cressida allowed herself to smile. Something strange flickered for a moment in the green depths of his eyes, but faded almost immediately as he said, 'I thought we might go out with your father's ashes straight after the service tomorrow. Is that what you want to do?'

'Yes.' She should be feeling grief, or pain; even a sense of loss would be preferable to this hollow in her heart when she thought of her father.

Luke's hand closed warmly, comfortingly, around her thin fingers. Tears ached at the back of her eyes. She said, 'I think I'll go to bed,' because she was going to cry with self-pity.

They said goodnight and she went out of the room, conscious of their watchful eyes on her rigid figure.

But she did not cry. Instead, she sat in the chair by the pretty little writing-desk and wondered forlornly what she was going to do.

CHAPTER THREE

THE NIGHT brought no counsel, no sudden inspiration, so that Cressida dressed in a cool grey morning with the dreary conviction that only time would help her. The thought of the memorial service that morning froze her emotions.

Luke was alone at the breakfast-table, drinking coffee with a frowning absorption which did not lift when Cressida came into the room, although he got to his feet with the bred-in-the-bone courtesy which she had noticed in him before. She knew that she was sallow, her eyes a dull opaque blue without the highlights which normally gave them character, so she was not surprised when his frown deepened.

'Sleep badly?' he asked.

At her nod he poured a glass of orange juice and passed it across to her. 'Drink that, it might help. I can't give you any glib comfort, I'm afraid, except that from my own experience I know that eventually the pain will go and you'll be able to remember him with joy and love.'

The voice of experience, hard-gained when his own father died, no doubt. Cressida couldn't tell him that all she could feel was a bleak emptiness, so she nodded and began on the bacon and eggs which had appeared on her plate, eating and drinking without tasting anything.

When at last she sat looking at her empty plate, Luke said gently, 'Be strong for a little longer,

Cressida.'

The service was soothing, the words and music and the honest compassion of those who were there helping to ease Cressida's misery. She accepted their sympathy with a secret reservation, wondering whether they would be so kind if they knew how little she could mourn for her father. After a small gathering at the homestead, they went away, and Cressida picked at some lunch, her face pinched and secretive. She felt a fraud.

So much so that Luke's voice made her jump and look warily at him. 'Come on, we'll go out now. Do you want Mother to come?'

'I—no, thank you.' To herself she thought, the fewer the better.

He nodded as though he understood, and held open the door for her.

If the inquest had been hard and the funeral service harder, this committal of her father's ashes to the element he had loved so much was unbearable. Luke took the *Windhover* out through the harbour entrance under engine and hove it to, bow into the waves. He came to stand beside Cressida while she tipped all that was mortal of her father into the heaving, cold waters, and threw after him a bunch of spring flowers which Mrs Scrivener had cut for her from the garden. They floated on the waste of the sea, their cheerful little heads one by one disappearing beneath the water while above a gull wailed a lonely lament.

Cressida shivered and turned blindly away, seeking the warmth of another human being, nuzzling compulsively into Luke's chest, her whole soul screaming her outrage at having to abandon her father to the impersonal sea, without ceremony, without one true mourner. It seemed to signify the wasteland her father's life had been in the end, with only a yacht and a shelf of books and a daughter who couldn't love him. So little to show for the years.

Hard arms tightened around her. Luke rested his cheek on her damp, wind-tossed tresses and said, 'Yes, cry, it will make you feel better. But not for this, because this is what he wanted.'

Cressida couldn't speak, her jaw aching with the rigid restraint she set upon herself. Luke's arms about her stiff figure were wonderfully warm; he moved so that her face was tucked warmly into his throat. He smelt of salt and the indescribable scent of male, warm and unfamiliar and comforting. For the first time in her life since childhood's blind trust, she felt protected, and knew in some deep instinctive part of her that such a feeling was dangerous. She began to shake and he tipped her head and looked long into her desolate face before he said gently, 'Go below, I'll take us back in.'

But she stood large-eyed and shivering beside him until he looped a casual arm over her shoulder and held her close to his big warm body until they reached the cove.

Once home Luke said crisply, 'You need something to warm you. Go and have a shower, and I'll send Mother up with a drink.'

She obeyed, even drank the hot toddy Mrs Scrivener bore up to her, but she refused to get into bed, saying desperately, 'No, I'll only lie there and think.'

'I know, my poor girl. Very well, then.'

When he saw her coming down the stairs, Luke frowned, but a quick glance from his mother warned him and he made no comment on Cressida's reappearance beyond a swift, searching look that noted the hollows under those proud cheekbones and the dark circles that still drained the colour from her eyes.

Mrs Scrivener poured tea and began to talk in a gentle, inexorable way which effectively diverted Cressida's mind. Good manners insisted that she respond, and after a few minutes the strain in her voice ebbed and she could feel colour warm her cheeks. That appalling frozen feeling was going; she no longer had to hold herself stiffly against the shivers which had threatened to rack her body.

After twenty minutes, Luke, who had been silent, said crisply, 'If you've drunk enough tea, Cressida, you can come out now for your first driving lesson.'

'No,' she protested, irritated by his high-handed disposition of her time. 'I'll help clear away here.'

But Mrs Scrivener said, 'It won't take me a moment to do this—you go with Luke, my dear.'

A spark of anger flared to life in her glance. She hesitated, then gave in, thinking apathetically that it was too much trouble to pit her will against his.

Half an hour later she was far from apathetic. Her hands felt all thumbs, her colour was riding high and her legs were oddly shaky, but under Luke's careful tutelage she had driven his enormous BMW through a gate and over a cattlestop, and then turned it around in the paddock and taken it back to the wide courtyard by the garage.

'Good,' he said calmly, surveying her stunned expression with lurking amusement. 'You should have your licence in no time. Come inside, I've a copy of the Road Code in the office somewhere. You might as well spend as much time as you can learning it by heart.'

In the days that followed, he bullied her gently into

constant practice, tested her on various aspects of the
Road Code and insisted that she drive out to the main
road each day to collect the mail with him. In between
she helped Mrs Scrivener and the housekeeper and
watched the spring unfold slowly, beautifully,
towards summer.

Life at Five Mile was always busy, yet peaceful.
Cressida learned to love the place and the pace,
discovering how the station was run, the never-ending
toil and the pleasure that came with a job well done.
Luke worked long hours outside, but the office was a
hard taskmaster and in spite of the secretary who
ruled there he spent many of his evenings at his desk.

His mother ran the house with the housekeeper's
assistance, but seemed to spend a lot of her time
acting as unpaid welfare officer for the people who
lived in the comfortable bungalows scattered around
the station. It was Mrs Scrivener who drove a terrified expectant mother into the cottage hospital when
she went early into labour and couldn't reach the
husband who had decided to go fishing on his day off,
and it was Mrs Scrivener who went with one of the
workers to the nearest office of the Inland Revenue
after he confessed that he hadn't filed a return for the
last two years. She gave moral support when another
couple were interviewed by the headmaster at the
local secondary school because one of their sons had
been suspended for smoking. Like her son's, her days
were full and busy and she obviously loved her life.
Cressida felt a kind of envy because she was so suited
to it, so happy.

On one level, Cressida was too. Her days also were
busy, but occasionally the constant presence of people
about her fretted at her nerves. She was not
accustomed to it; her life with her father had neces-

sarily been a lonely one for much of the time, and although she had longed to give it up she found now that she had enjoyed the solitude more than she realised.

And she rather thought that her incipient crush on Luke had developed into fullblown maturity. Each evening, she found herself waiting for him to come inside, listening for his footsteps with the sudden vital surge of excitement which he roused. So carefully that he rarely caught her, she watched him from beneath her lashes, imprinting on her mind the contours of his body, the wide muscled torso which tapered to lean waist and hips, the long limbs and proud, poised head. And other, less obvious things; his elegant economy of movement and gesture, the way the hard severity of his features could be softened by a fleeting tenderness, the lift of his chin when he teased her and the mocking gleam in his eye when she flashed back at him.

Cressida watched him as though she had never seen a man before, and she had to fight hard to dampen down the unbidden incandescent exhilaration he aroused in her.

Because there were women in his life. One called Paula Radford, in particular, who seemed to know all about Cressida and who spoke with a drawling super-confident voice when she rang Luke. Which happened at least twice a week.

'She's a lawyer in Auckland,' Mrs Scrivener confided one night when Luke took the call, as he always did, in the office. 'The daughter of one of my dearest friends. She is, unfortunately, devoted to her work.'

'Unfortunately?'

The older woman smiled ruefully. 'Yes. There's no

scope for her up here, and I'm afraid anyone who marries Luke is going to have to give up most of her life to the station.'

Jealousy, Cressida discovered, can pierce like a sword to the heart. She had to wait a second until she was able to say quietly, 'Perhaps Miss Radford would be prepared to compromise?'

'Paula? No, she's not the compromising sort. And I don't see how she could. Can you imagine Luke putting up with a part-time wife? I don't know what they're going to do, because they're very fond of each other, they've been going out together for years. There have been others, but I'm sure they were only diversions.' She caught herself up a little guiltily and went on with brisk care, 'A big station like Five Mile must have a full-time mistress, and Luke is all man, he needs a woman who can give all of herself. It's so very sad; feminism is a wonderful movement and I'm all for it, but I can't help feeling that it works best in cities! Once you get a situation like this, somebody has to be prepared to sacrifice their career.'

Cressida nodded, remembering her mother, who had given up all that she held dear, caught in the sweet trap that was love. Had it been worthwhile for her? She would never know now.

The call was short, for at that moment Luke came in through the door, his jaw set. His mother sent Cressida a warning look and went on with her knitting, asking placidly after Paula.

'You'll be able to see for yourself soon,' he said briefly. 'She's coming up for a weekend.'

Diane Scrivener beamed. 'How lovely! It's been months since I saw her. Is she driving up?'

'Yes.' He looked across at Cressida and the glitter in his eyes softened. 'You look like a little owl, all eyes.

Why don't you go to bed?'

And that, she thought rather despondently, certainly put her in her place. She got to her feet and said her goodnights, and left the room to the sound of her hostess's voice, eagerly suggesting treats for Paula Radford.

After she had showered, she pulled on the thin shirt which she slept in and sat wearily on the side of her bed, brushing her hair with unnecessary vigour as she tried to reason herself out of her despondency. First love was notorious for this sort of thing, she had read enough books to know that. They had all stated that it hurt, too. What they hadn't said was that, when in its throes, one could feel a pain little short of anguish, and a bitter blazing jealousy that terrified its unfortunate recipient.

Cressida was still trying hard to compose herself when there was a knock at the door. After a moment spent staring at it, she got up to answer it.

'Oh,' she said half-beneath her breath when she saw Luke almost filling the doorway.

He commanded crisply, 'Put on your dressing-gown. There's something I have to talk to you about.'

'I haven't got a dressing-gown.'

His eyes drifted down her body to the slender tanned length of her legs and then back up. Something dark gleamed in their depths for a moment there, but he said in a mild enough voice, 'Then put something a little less interesting over the top of that outfit, will you?'

Cressida turned away hastily and dragged on jeans and a jersey, her skin still smarting from that leisurely survey. 'Come in,' she invited politely, waving at the chair.

Luke waited until she was sitting in the only other

chair, that by the writing-desk, then sat down and said without preamble, 'I've just been talking to Sam Thorburn. He said that he's had word from your father's agent in London, and that he had contracted with his publishers to get another manuscript ready for them by the end of this year. Do you know anything about it?'

'Yes. We came down to New Zealand because it will soon be the hurricane season in the islands. My father wanted to spend the summer in the Bay of Islands working on it.'

'How? His books are a combination of travel story and philosophical treatise. Did he take notes, work from tapes . . .?'

'He kept very full diaries,' Cressida told him. 'And notes—he'd think of something and scribble it on one of the pieces of paper that he always carried in his pockets. Then he had to get them in some sort of order. It takes—took—him about four months to get a manuscript ready.'

He nodded, his gaze watchful. 'The publishers want that book. Is there anybody who could complete it?'

'No,' she said, wondering what he meant. She hesitated, then said thoughtfully, 'Well, I suppose anyone could use his diaries, but it wouldn't be the same.'

'The publishers suggested that you might be able to.'

'No! Oh, no!' She jumped to her feet, almost huddling away from him, as though he had just made an obscene suggestion. For a second her face was stark and rigid with rejection. She turned her head away, trying to hide from his unsparing gaze.

'I didn't realise that you'd had a book published,' said Luke.

Cressida shook her head. 'It was just a—just a one-off thing, travels in the Mediterranean seen through the eyes of a child. It was really just a joke.' Her voice faltered. She finished, 'My mother helped me a lot with it.'

'I see. Nevertheless, your father's publishers would like to see if you can do something with your father's manuscript. When I had the yacht stripped, I put all of his papers away in the office. I'll get them out.'

Like a cornered cat she turned on him, teeth bared. 'I don't want to do anything with them, damn you! Leave them alone! Or parcel them up and send them to the publisher. Let them do what they want to with them, I don't care if I never see them again. Just forget about them and leave me alone!'

Luke stood up too, suddenly forbidding and as angry as she was. With brutal emphasis he returned, 'You can't just turn your back on life. It's cowardly and spineless and useless.'

'I never pretended to be anything but,' she flashed back.

His lips tightened into a narrow, forbidding line. 'Don't be a fool. I'll see that you get them tomorrow. You can look at them and then decide what to do with them in a logical manner, free from this silly emotionalism.'

'I will not!'

He said nothing, just looked at her, his eyes compelling and merciless, and after a long tense moment she said in a drained voice, 'Very well.'

For some reason he was still angry, she could sense it, but he controlled it and said with cool kindness, 'I think you'll find that I'm right, Cressida.'

That was when she knew that she would have to go. She nodded, and he watched her for a second longer before turning and leaving, but although her eyes followed him through the door she didn't really see him.

He was just like her father, strong enough to impose his will on her, and arrogant enough to be convinced that his was the only way. What was it about her that made her spineless, so easily intimidated? Weakness, she decided miserably. She was weak and without the stamina to stand up to him. Life simply wasn't fair. Not only had it seen to it that she grew up with a man who subordinated the needs of his family to an obsession, but fate had ensured that she waste her first love on yet another autocratic male.

She would have to go; she could not bear to stay in love with a man who treated her as if her wishes were of no account.

But not yet. Although Sam Thorburn had sent her an advance big enough to buy a few clothes locally, mainly jeans and shirts and jerseys, her father's estate was still not probated. She had no real money. No money, no home and no skills.

A dreary little litany of negatives, but at the moment only the last item worried her. Although she had no idea of the size of her father's estate, she did know that very few writers made much from their vocation. But even if he had left enough to keep her she would have to find a job. Obscurely she felt that it would be unbearable to be supported by her father; if she did use his money she was allowing him to dictate to her from the grave. Irrational such a conviction might be, but it was rooted in her innermost being.

The next morning, she broached the subject of her lack of marketable skills to Mrs Scrivener.

The older woman regarded her guest's earnest, too-thin face thoughtfully. 'I'm afraid I'm not sure what we can do about it, Cresida. Did you have anything in mind?'

Cressida shook her head, feeling even more useless. 'No, that's the trouble. Some people have a vocation, but I haven't.'

'What were you good at at school?'

A fleeting mischief transformed Cressida's features. 'Maths and physics.'

'Goodness, how clever of you, my dear! Did you have any hopes of a career?'

The mischief fled, replaced by a desolation which lasted only a second. With carefully schooled features, she replied, 'No. Oh, I thought perhaps I might go on to university, but my father wanted me to be his crew.'

'I see.' Mrs Scrivener's voice was without inflection, but Cressida had the feeling that she really did see. However, she said nothing more on the subject, for which Cressida was thankful.

Instead, practical as always, she resumed, 'I think we should have a look around and see what can be done. There are correspondence schools, and courses you can take at technical institutes. You'll have to wait until the beginning of the educational year to take up anything like that, though, which is after Christmas. Shall I get Luke's secretary to find out?'

'I can do it.' It was important that Cressida take up the reins of her own life, and her mien showed it. 'If you can tell me where to get the addresses . . .?'

'The Auckland telephone directory. I'll scribble down all the ones whose names I can recall, shall I? That will give you something to go on.'

Cressida gave her a fugitive smile and thanked her earnestly before taking herself off to the kitchen, where Mrs Collins was going to show her how to make a never-fail soufflé. Half an hour later, she was watching the glass oven door with anxiety when Luke came in, frowning as he saw her.

'Hiding, Cressida?'

Flatly she retorted, 'No, I'm not. I've just made the soufflé for lunch and I'm watching it rise, so don't stamp your foot or shout.'

He grinned and joined her in her vigil, standing beside her as the mixture rose and stiffened. She felt stifled; he was so big that, even in the huge kitchen, designed to make it easy to prepare food for big parties as well as just the family, he seemed to take up more than his share of room.

'It looks perfect,' he said, sounding surprised.

Mrs Collins bristled a little. 'Well, what did you expect? Not only am I an exceptional cook, I'm a good teacher. Not that there's a lot I can teach this young lady, she's pretty good herself.'

'My father liked good meals,' Cressida said drily, even though her cheeks pinked at the praise.

Or perhaps it was the fact that Luke was watching her with amusement and something else, something she didn't recognise in those strange tawny-green eyes.

'Do you want to take it in yourself?'

Cressida laughed at the housekeeper's question. 'Yes, please, then if it falls flat as a paving stone you won't have to take the blame.'

'It won't.' Mrs Collins was quite unperturbed.

'I'll just go up and wash the flour off my face,' Cressida decided, seizing the opportunity to leave the kitchen.

But Luke came with her, and on the way up the stairs said with calm authority, 'I'll see you in the office after lunch.'

Which effectively spoiled any appetite she had. She shot him a swift, frustrated glance, which was met by a perfectly pleasant but steely one in return. With something very close to a flounce, she went into her room.

Miserable, because in spite of the anger that prickled her skin her stupid heart was throbbing double time in her breast, she washed her perfectly clean face and ran a comb through her hair, and was horrified to catch herself staring at her reflection, trying to see herself as others saw her. No, as *he* saw her.

Scolding herself for being a fool, she jerked away, but in her mind she could see her face, a little thin, still with some of the tan she had gained in the tropics, the cheekbones stark beneath large dark eyes. They were so dark, those eyes, and so thickly lashed in black, that people sometimes exclaimed in surprise when they realised that they were blue. From surreptitious reading of glossy magazines, Cressida knew that she didn't fit into any stereotype of feminine beauty, but she rather thought she had good bone structure and she was lucky with her skin.

The rest of her was more or less normal. Not very tall, but not short, and slim, with hips that curved a little too much, to match her breasts, which were also a little too large. Uninspiring, she thought gloomily, and although she knew she was begging for trouble, she wasted a minute or so dreaming of a miraculous trans-formation which would bring Luke to his knees.

How was it possible to want a man who was bad for you? Frowning fearsomely, she told herself that this was not love, a crush was just physical attraction. It hurt, the books all said so, but you got over it. They all said that, too.

'Roll on the day,' she said, on what was meant to be a frivolous note; it was a pity that her voice broke on the last word.

The soufflé was a success, high and delicious and succulent, and Cressida smiled as she was congratulated by Luke and his mother. Then she sat quietly, picking at it, while they discussed a distant cousin whose daughter was getting married 'not before time', as Mrs Scrivener put it, looking significantly at her son.

He winked at Cressida and said in the blandest of voices, 'I believe my father was thirty-four when he finally married you.'

'He didn't *finally* marry me!' Mrs Scrivener looked crossly at him. 'Really, Luke, what an extraordinary way of putting things!'

'When he finally met you,' Luke corrected. 'Met you and fell in love with you and swept you off your feet. Is that more like it?'

'Yes, it is, and you're not to tease me or think you can evade the subject quite so easily! I'd like a few grandchildren to dandle on my knee before I die.'

'Ask Sally and Tom to oblige you,' Luke advised generously.

'Your sister is just as wary as you are, at least of having children. Still, I have hopes. In her last letter, she sounded a little bored with her life. I know she and Tom have to stay in Los Angeles for another three years, and they weren't planning on having children until they came back home, but I think she might change her mind.'

'It will give her something to do,' Luke agreed carelessly. He drained the last of his tea and looked across the table at Cressida. 'Ready?'

Mutiny sparked her eyes to brightest, richest sapphire, but she got to her feet obediently enough and excused herself.

'Good girl,' he said, so much indulgence in his tone that she felt like slapping him.

She said nothing, however, until they were inside the office and she was looking at the box on the desk. Then she said despairingly, 'This has to be the craziest idea I've ever heard! I can't do it.'

'Can't? Or won't?'

'Can't, damn you!' She turned away, but not before Luke saw the sheen of tears glimmering in her eyes.

His expression softened, but there was no sign of it in his voice, which was pointed and implacable. 'At the very least, you can arrange his papers in some sort of order. Then you can type the notes up.'

'I can't type.'

'Marie Collins will give you an hour's tuition a day.' He lifted a dark eyebrow at her surprise and went on, 'She was a commercial teacher until she married Ian. She was quite right when she said she was a good teacher.'

Cressida should have been pleased—this, after all, was what she had wanted. So why was she resentful? And why, when she looked at Luke, did her blood flow in a strange heavy beat through her veins? Unable to cope with it, she said in a goaded voice, 'Thank you very much for taking the trouble.'

'It was no trouble,' he said, laughing at her with his eyes. 'My mother asked Marie about various types of training, and when she realised who it was that was asking, and what you wanted, she offered.'

Trembling with temper, Cressida said in a small, prim voice, 'It's very kind of her. How much will she charge?'

The amusement vanished from his voice as if she

had hit him. He took her chin and lifted it with fingers which were just short of painful and said, 'That's quite enough of that, thank you. Marie offered, and you're not going to insult her by offering to pay her. Do you hear me?'

He was very formidable, the colour of his eyes a hard, pitiless green, and she was afraid. Her tongue touched the centre of her suddenly dry lip, but from somewhere she got the courage to reply huskily, 'Yes, I hear you, you don't need to shout at me.'

Something flared in Luke's eyes. It was swiftly hidden by the sudden descent of his lashes, but not before she realised with a strange kind of excitement that he had been watching the little movement of her tongue and the way her lips shaped the sulky words, and that he had responded to such a small thing.

He had not wanted to, which was why he was releasing her now and saying in a tone which was meant to relegate her to the schoolroom, 'Very well, then. Marie will be ready at half-past three. Why don't you start sorting through these papers?'

Something fiery and painful twisted inside Cressida. For the first time in her life she understood the power and the limitations of physical passion. The traitor within her body was taunting her with images of Luke's arms closing around her, of her body imprisoned against his, of his cruel, potent mouth making him master of her responses. Yet, at the same moment, she wanted nothing more than to yell defiance at him, hit him so that he was forced to accept her as a person, not a child to be ordered about.

Even in her most mutinous moods she had never felt such a tempest of emotion for her father. An instinct she didn't know she possessed was warning her that the very force of her response was a danger, because Luke was not indifferent to her. For a moment there he had wanted her, and she had recognised his desire and gloried in it.

She said nervously, 'Yes, all right,' praying that he would leave her alone, go away before she made a complete and utter fool of herself.

'Cressida?'

Reluctantly she looked up at him, masking her expression, willing herself to reveal nothing of the turmoil of her thoughts. A crush, she told herself desperately. Just a common-or-garden case of infatuation. It happened to everyone in adolescence.

Although Luke was smiling, his face was almost impassive, yet at that moment she felt she knew how the Vikings had looked when they set out on one of their wild forays. She said huskily, 'Yes?'

'Don't dislike me too much,' he said wryly, and left the room.

Alone at last, she stared for long moments down at the polished surface of the desk, her mind a maelstrom. Then, shivering as though faced by a peril beyond all reckoning, she walked around to the big chair and sat down. For the moment, the emotions which Luke roused in her protected her from the discomfort she felt at reading the scraps of paper on which her father had written his thoughts.

Not for long, however. As she smoothed the papers out, she thought how strange it was that her father, that most tidy of men, should choose to be so disorganised with the work which enabled him to lead the life he wanted.

And before very long she was lost in the task, not making much of an effort to sort things, just reading and remembering.

Her eyes were wet when Mrs Collins put her head

around the door.

'Afternoon tea time,' that lady said succinctly, adding, 'You look as though you need it. There are visitors, but I can bring your tea in here if you don't want to meet them.'

'Oh, no, thank you.' Encouraged by the older woman's sympathy, Cressida got to her feet, looking down in dismay at the wild tangle of papers spread out across the desk. 'I can't leave this here. Is there a table I could put in my bedroom so that I can work on things there?'

'Bound to be, in the attic if nowhere else. Leave it to me, I'll find one.'

Cressida smiled. 'I'll help you.'

Normally they all drank tea in the morning-room off the kichen, but today it was to be served in the small drawing-room. Cressida liked the old-fashioned names for the rooms, just as she liked the rooms themselves, big and high-ceilinged with picture rails and dados still intact, and in many of them the delicate pressed tin ceilings which set the homestead indisputably in the Victorian era. Perhaps because only one family had lived in the house, there had been no drastic modernisation; the kitchen and bathrooms were miracles of modern plumbing, but they had been altered with tact and finesse.

And although Cressida knew very little about antiques she had visited enough museums to understand that the furniture in the homestead would make an antique dealer drool with lust.

Just outside the door she hesitated. 'Perhaps I should change,' she suggested, looking down at her workaday jeans and the warm primrose jersey above them.

'Nonsense, you look lovely. These are nice normal

women, my dear, with daughters who run around like that all the time!' Marie gave her a bracing smile. 'You're the celebrity.'

Which was not a comforting thought to take with her into the room, but Cressida held her head high and summoned up her most cheerful smile.

Of course, the housekeeper had been right. Although the two women who were introduced to her hid any curiosity they may have felt and were pleasant, the daughter of one of them, Fiona Mason, was very much more open in her attitude. She eyed Cressida with such blatant interest that her mother frowned and Mrs Scrivener deftly led the conversation into other channels.

A little later, when the three older women were discussing a fund-raising effort to build a new swimming pool for the local primary school, Fiona slipped an adroit question into a convenient gap, asking politely if she and Cressida could go to see the horses. She was dying to see the new foals.

'Of course,' Mrs Scrivener agreed, after a swift questioning glance at Cressida's smooth face.

In five minutes, the two girls were making their way across the back yard to a gate in the hedge which led out on to the drive and thence past the assortment of sheds holding machinery and equipment and stores for the station.

'I suppose you find life here a little dull after all the excitement of sailing around the world,' Fiona said enviously. She had an odd little trick of hesitating before words she wanted to emphasise, so her comments came out as if she had to gasp for air.

'No, I like it very much. I've never lived on a farm before.'

Fiona looked about her with a disparaging expression. 'Well, I was born and brought up on a farm, so it's nothing new for me, but if I had to live on one I must admit I'd choose the one Luke owns.' She sighed luxuriously, peeping at Cressida from beneath knowing lids. 'Isn't he just the most gorgeous man you've ever met? Honestly, when he smiles he makes my toes go all funny, right up my legs and into my backbone!'

Cressida had to laugh. 'He's certainly handsome,' she agreed, a little cautiously.

Another heavy sigh, as Fiona lifted her eyes heavenward. 'Handsome is hardly the word! You know, I've never been able to work out just why he's so attractive, and believe me, I've tried! I mean, you see any number of handsome men, but I've never come across one who has the same effect on women as Luke. One smile and we all go weak at the knees!'

'Don't I know it, Cressida thought wryly, but instinct warned her that Fiona was not a safe person to confide in, so she made a noncommittal noise and waited.

'I've finally come to the conclusion that it's because you don't know what's lurking behind that stunning face. I've never known him to be anything but unfailingly polite and very cool, very controlled, but I always get the feeling that all that restraint is very necessary because underneath he's absolutely seething with passion. Don't you think so?'

Although she wouldn't have put it in quite the same way, Cressida was surprised to find that she understood exactly what her companion meant. Somehow, in spite of the formidable reserve he could summon when he wanted to, it was very easy to see Luke as a man of passions so strong that they needed the curb of his will to hold them in check. Easy, and disturbing.

In a voice she tried hard to keep level she murmured, 'Do you think so?'

'Well,' Fiona said cosily, revealing herself for a born gossip, 'I happen to know that he has the most appalling temper. Apparently, when he was young, about fifteen or so, he nearly killed one of the men who worked here. I don't know the story—Mr Scrivener, Luke's father, hushed it all up—but I did hear that Luke took to him with a batten of wood and smashed him into a pulp because he beat his wife when he found that she was having an affair with Luke!'

Cressida sorted out this somewhat tangled account with ease. She was intelligent enough to discount most of what she heard, knowing from her days at school how easily rumours gained credence, but even so she was sickened by the relish with which the other girl relayed the gossip, making it into a sordid little tale.

'Sounds unlikely,' she managed to say with every appearance of unconcern, aware of Fiona's sharp gaze fixed on her face. 'I mean, fifteen-year-old boys don't usually go in for affairs with married women, do they? It seems awfully precocious.'

'I've seen a photo of him at fifteen,' said Fiona, shuddering with ostentatious pleasure. 'He looked like a young god. Adonis—no, one of the Norse gods. That hint of violence behind the stunning face.' She darted another quick look up at Cressida's shuttered expression, then sighed, languorously and to great effect. 'Not that it's any use us dreaming about him, alas, not when Paula Radford is the lady in occupation, so to speak. They've been having a flaming affair for years now. Mum says that if she were Paula she wouldn't keep him waiting for too long. When she finally gives up being liberated, she might find that Luke's found someone else to marry. Men are still not all that keen on clever women, are they? And really, a place like Five Mile needs a woman who was born and bred in the country.'

Cressida said sweetly, 'I thought Mrs Scrivener came here as a bride from Auckland.'

'Well, yes, but in those days women did, didn't they?' Not at all abashed by Cressida's bemused response to this piece of ambiguity, Fiona gurgled with laughter before elaborating, 'Follow their men, I mean. You know, whither thou goest . . . The world well lost for love . . . and all that.'

'Oh, I see.' Yes, in those days women did. Cressida's mind flew to her memories of her mother.

'Hey, where have you gone?' Fiona trilled a little artificial laugh and tossed her head, suddenly very vivacious, her eyes sparkling in a manner which astonished Cressida. She went on effusively, 'There, aren't they the most gorgeous little things? I do love foals, don't you, Cressy?'

'Ah—yes.' Cressida was too irritated by the arbitrary shortening of her name to make any more than a lukewarm rejoinder, but as Fiona laughed again and chided her playfully for her lack of enthusiasm she realised what had brought on this attack of vivacity.

Luke, mounted on his favourite gelding, a magnificent grey called Blue, was riding up to the fence, followed as always by a brace of dogs. His smile was a white slash in his tanned face; he reined in and swung down, looping the reins over the nearest post. The foals, who had been persuaded by mischief and curiosity towards the two girls, took flight and galloped in their charmingly awkward fashion to the shelter of their placid mothers, who swished their tails and watched the gelding through the fence with wary eyes.

Cressida gave an involuntary chuckle and followed Fiona over the grass to meet Luke.

What followed was as interesting to Cressida as it was embarrassing. Apparently she was not the only one to have a crush on Luke; Fiona's comments had prepared her, but it wasn't until she saw the other girl's blush as Luke smiled at her that she understood fully.

But poor Fiona wasn't able to hide her emotions; as if compelled, she bent all her attention to the man who kept her at a distance by treating her with the charming but aloof manner of a mature man for a schoolgirl.

Cressida admired him for that. Without trying, she was finding Fiona very irritating. She was so silly! she thought scornfully, and then, horrified, perhaps that's how I seem to him. But no, she didn't simper at him, or flutter her eyelashes or try to monopolise his attention as Fiona was doing.

Although there was amusement in his eyes when he spoke to the infatuated girl, there was understanding and a touch of compassion, too. To her astonishment, Cressida discovered that she liked him immensely. And that was dangerous. Lust was one thing; liking was more difficult to cope with. Liking could lead to love.

She was silent all the way back to the house.

CHAPTER FOUR

AFTER Fiona had driven their visitors away in a gratuitous splatter of gravel which summoned apprehensive looks to the faces of the two older women in the car, Mrs Scrivener asked interestedly, 'What did you think of her?'

'She seems awfully young.' Cressida weighed her words before answering; she was relieved at the chuckle they provoked.

'She's a nice thing really, just like her mother, all gossip and good works, which is wearing but, I suppose, better than being no gossip and no good works. As you may have noticed, she has a crush on Luke.'

'She doesn't actually hide it,' said Cressida drily.

'Well,' Mrs Scrivener observed judiciously, 'I think she tries, poor child. Still, she'll grow out of it. You may also have noticed that he doesn't encourage her.'

Luke had come in with them, made pleasant conversation with his mother's visitors for ten minutes or so, and then left them, pretending not to see the appeal in Fiona's gaze as she protested. After that, she had lost any pretence of interest in the proceedings, ignoring her mother's attempts to coax her into the conversation to stare longingly out of the window towards the horse paddock.

'She's been spoiled, of course, but basically she's a nice girl. I'd hoped she might be a friend for you.'

Mrs Scrivener smiled at Cressida's embarrassment. 'I should have known better, even from my great age I can remember how I hated it when my mother tried to pick friends for me. And you're such a mature thing, Fiona would seem childish to you.'

'I didn't say that!' Perturbed, Cressida lifted her gaze to meet the shrewd eyes twinkling at her.

'No, but that's what you meant, and of course you're right, she is young for her age. Now, I think Luke wants to see you in the office.'

With a profound sense of reluctance, Cressida went to knock on the door, entering at Luke's call. He was leaning against the desk, frowning slightly as he sorted through a sheaf of papers, his stance emphasising the sheer dominance so characteristic of him, grace and strength combined into a physical presence which caught the attention of everyone about him. Cressida's nerves tightened. He looked up, meeting her wary smile with a disconcertingly cool survey.

'Marie tells me you want a table to work on,' he said. At her nod he went on, 'Do I take it from that that you've decided to do the job?'

'No, I've decided to get my father's diaries into order, that's all. I'm not capable of writing his book.'

Luke lifted his brows, but said nothing. After a further moment spent perusing them, he put the papers into the leather briefcase standing open beside him.

'That, I suppose, will do for now,' he said, looking up to catch her staring. He waited until her blush had faded before asking blandly, 'Did you enjoy yourself this afternoon?'

Cressida returned with a snap, 'Do you think I'm a freak or something? I can enjoy civilised company.'

For some reason, she wanted to provoke him; there was a pleasure in quarrelling with him which came close to the exhilarating recklessness of danger. Her eyes glittered, burning sapphire beneath a sweep of lashes more provocative than the open challenge in her voice.

But he grinned, very shrewd and pointed, refusing to rise to her bait. In tones which held enough mockery to puncture her bravado, he said, 'I'm sorry if we've given you that impression. It's just that occasionally you seem to find yourself feeling a little trapped, and Fiona can be overpowering.'

He must have kept a very close watch on her to notice her occasional moments of paranoia, her need for space. Uneasy because his very perception brought a recurrence of that caged feeling, she replied, 'I do, but it's not—I can go for a walk or to my room and be alone for a while, and it goes.

Luke watched her for a moment longer, his eyes enigmatic, then he picked up another sheaf of papers, riffling through them with a faint frown drawing his brows together. Cressida watched the lean fingers, dark against the white paper, while a strange heat ached in the pit of her stomach.

When he spoke again she jumped, and he frowned at her, his glance probing. 'Marie is going to find you a table, and her husband will put it into your room. I'm leaving in a few minutes for Wellington.'

Which explained the briefcase. Fighting to ignore a sudden hollowness in her heart, she commented casually, 'Wellington is a long way away.'

'It's the capital,' he said, shrugging. 'I'm on a committee of advice to the government. We meet once a month, and tomorrow is the day. I'll spend tonight in Auckland, then catch the businessman's special down in the morning. I should be back by Thursday.'

Cressida smiled—what else was there to do?—and said inanely, 'Have a good time.'

'Well, it will be interesting,' he said, and came around the desk to give her a teasing smile. 'Come out to the airstrip with me and I'll let you drive the Land Rover back.'

As he intended, she blenched. For safety reasons, the airstrip had been formed on a ridge some distance from the homestead. It was ideal for the purpose, providing a long sweep of grassy flat eminently suitable for the Cessna he owned and the topdressing planes which used it, but the only track wound its way up from the valley without much in the way of bulwarks against a drop which became progressively more precipitous.

'I'll come out with you,' she said, 'but I won't bring the Land Rover back.'

For a moment, she thought Luke was going to insist, and sheer panic set her jaw in a rigid line until a quick glance upwards showed that there was nothing but a rather mocking amusement in his expression.

Boldly she announced, 'You're a beast! I'll bet you tormented the life out of your sister when you were children!'

'Never. She gave me hell—a thoroughly frightening girl. You wait until you meet her.'

No, Cressida thought that night as she got ready for bed, he did not seem the sort of man who would have an affair with a married woman, or beat a man almost to death. Not even in his youth, before that control had had time to become an integral part of his nature. Fiona must have been exaggerating.

Yet Cressida couldn't help remembering the sheer pleasure in Luke's face as he had fought the wind and the sea to bring *Windhover* in through the heads. He had revelled in his own daring, his recklessness, freed from the bonds of civilised restraint.

Without him the days dragged, and then, an hour before he was due back on Thursday, he rang to tell his mother that he had decided to stay an extra night in Auckland and bring Paula up with him after she finished work the next night.

'I thought they might do that,' Mrs Scrivener said, obviously pleased. 'It's only sensible, it will save her driving both ways. Now she always goes into the room next to Luke's. I'll just put the sheets on.'

It was painful, but courtesy dictated that Cressida offer to help.

'No, thank you, dear, but if you'd like to, how about ransacking the garden tomorrow afternoon and picking some flowers to go in both rooms? Something striking for Paula's room, she's such a dramatic character, and whatever you like for Luke.'

So, the next day, Cressida picked three crimson waratah flowers, their cones held in wiry splendour above the glowing bracts which formed a frill at the base, and with the aid of a flat black lacquer dish and a cream striped ribbon of flax leaf made an arrangement which was Japanese in inspiration.

For Luke she chose freesias and grape hyacinths and the vivid blue flowers of Dutch irises, arranging them in a country style, artfully informal.

'Lovely,' Mrs Scrivener said generously. 'Could you take them up? I can hear the phone ringing.'

Carefully, Cressida carried them up the stairs, first the waratahs which she delivered to the red and white bedroom and then the spring bowl. It felt strange to be going into Luke's bedroom; she had never seen more of it than the door. With the bowl in her hands, she surveyed the big room, her eyes widening as she imagined Luke in it.

It was surprisingly spare of furniture, almost austere, although the bed was an enormous four-poster with a cover of deep dark green, the colour of a black emerald. Curtains of the same shade fell on either side of the big double-hung windows; there was an antique French desk and a chair and a magnificent *armoire*. On one wall, the stark lines of a superb modern lithograph were balanced by what had to be a copy of a cartoon bearing the unmistakable impress of Leonardo da Vinci.

Altogether an unexpected mixture of traditional and contemporary, Cressida mused as she took the flowers across to the desk. She wondered if Luke had had anything to do with the decorating, or whether his mother had done it for him. It was a room for a man who enjoyed comfort yet had a puritan streak, she decided, and wondered if she was being fanciful.

'They look perfect.' Mrs Scrivener's voice made her jump. 'You really do have a talent for flowers. I'm sure that, if you wanted to, you could get a job in a florist's shop.'

'I might have to do that,' Cressida told her gloomily. 'My fingers are never going to be able to cope with a keyboard.'

'Rome wasn't built in a day. Marie thinks you're doing rather well. All that practising has to get you somewhere!'

'Sore fingers.'

'Well, let's go on down, and we'll have a cup of tea while we wait for them.'

They heard the plane come in just after dark, and after what seemed to a nervous Cressida to be an age there came the sound of the Land Rover as Marie's husband brought them back in. She had put on her best dress, a rather childish affair of pink cotton. Compared to the unknown Paula, she expected to be completely overshadowed. It did nothing for her confidence.

However, although she had been prepared for stunning beauty, she had not realised that Paula Radford was one those rare creatures endowed by an unfair fate with all of the assets; intelligence, a breathtaking symmetry of form and feature, and, as she discovered in the first five minutes, a genuinely nice nature.

'I'm glad to meet you,' Paula said when they were introduced, smiling with unstudied charm. 'Luke has been telling me all about you. I'm sorry about your father; it must have been a terrible experience, but Luke said you've been incredibly courageous.'

Cressida shot a furious look a Luke, which was met with his blandest stare, then blushed and only just prevented herself from hanging her head and muttering some idiotic rejoinder. She managed to say a little shortly, 'Courage didn't come into it, but it's kind of him to say so.'

Paula bestowed another smile on her and was instantly swept into the drawing-room, where a fire had been lit.

'Unless you'd rather go upstairs and change?' Mrs Scrivener asked.

'No, no, I'd love to warm up a little—I'm quite chilly. I'm not coming up by plane again until Luke installs a heater in the Land Rover.'

This was apparently an old joke; she tossed a sparkling glance at the man who was beside her, and he chuckled, his mouth curved in affection. Cressida felt a chill as old as time sweep through her, a chill of the spirit, that of being the outsider.

Then Luke looked across at her and his eyes grew
hooded; a moment later he said lightly, 'What can I
get you all to drink? Cressida, come and help me. It's
time you learned what goes into the making of a good
drink.'

'You shouldn't be encouraging her to drink, Luke.
She's too young, surely.' Paula's voice was faintly
admonitory.

Luke said calmly, 'So far, we've only managed to
coax her into drinking mineral water.'

'Wise girl.' Paula allowed herself to be drawn over
to the fire by her hostess, while Luke escorted
Cressida the few feet to the drinks tray.

'What is it?' he asked, not softly as though he didn't
want the others to hear, just quietly enough so that
they couldn't.

She made the mistake of evading the question. 'I
don't understand.'

His brows drew together and he sent her a level
stare, hard and sharp. As he poured glowing sherry
into a crystal glass he said curtly, 'You looked forlorn.
How have things been going?'

'Fine.' Purposely airy, she smiled. 'No problems.
Marie has proved to be a very gentle taskmaster.'

His frowned deepened and he said impatiently, 'Is
that the only dress you've got? It makes you look
about fifteen.'

Hurt, she retorted, 'I'm not all that much older.'

The irritation intensified; for a moment, the strong
bones of his face were stark with pressure, but even as
she watched it faded and he gave her a wry smile. 'At
your tender age, my girl, three years is a big step.
Now, why don't you take this across to my mother?'

Cressida did as she was told, for all the world like

the schoolgirl he compared her to, rebellion seething in her heart. When she looked at Paula, however, it died into ashes, cold and depressing. It was obvious why he had been so scathing about her pink dress. The older woman was dressed exquisitely in a black suit which revealed her reed slenderness to perfection; her shirt was chalky silk, and above it her mouth glowed a vivid red. It was a dramatic, severely simple outfit, with the gloss of a couturier's art, and it suited Paula's striking good looks superbly.

It was not the most auspicious start to an evening which grew rapidly worse. Cressida had braced herself for pain, expected it and had thought herself prepared for it, but nothing could prepare her for the bitter ache in her heart at the evidence of the intimacy between Paula and Luke.

Not that they were obvious about the fact that they were lovers. They were not. It was revealed in their complete understanding of each other, the total lack of self-consciousness between them.

It did not make it any easier for Cressida that they didn't stare sensuously at each other; she was sophisticated enough to know that desire was fairly common coinage in the world. What hurt her was the shared jokes, the moments when their eyes met and something passed between them so swiftly that it was almost imperceptible, the total confidence with which Paula treated him.

No, they didn't have to proclaim that they were lovers, that they loved each other. It was there in everything they said, everything they did, like a bond between them which nothing could ever break.

Cressida's heart twisted. Why did it have to happen like this? Paula was talking about some aspect of her work, and her pleasure in it was strong in her voice, her expression; Cressida's eyes moved to where Luke sat, a glass in his hand, the strong features locked into an impassive cast. Did it hurt him to know that he couldn't have her entirely? Cressida could have wept for him.

But he looked up before she had time to tear her eyes away and something changed in his eyes; the brooding quality metamorphosed into something she didn't recognise, and he smiled, a smile of sudden rare sweetness, and she went under without any fight at all.

Marie had surpassed herself with dinner; it was a pity that the rack of lamb and succulent scallops went untasted in Cressida's mouth, the delicious crispness of the salad unsavoured. She ate mandarin mousse without appreciating the contrast between sweet creaminess and the sharp tang of the citrus, and although she normally enjoyed the coffee that always finished the meal that, too, went unheeded.

She rather thought she behaved normally; she didn't miss any cues when it came to conversation and even, because she felt it her duty, entertained Paula with a short insight into her life as her father's crew. Discarding their rounding of Cape Horn as not colourful enough, she told how she and her father had stumbled on a millionaire's hideaway on a tiny island in the Pacific, hundreds of miles from anywhere, not realising until she finished that her cool voice revealed her distaste for the man who had gloried in the contrast between his opulent life-style and the simple dignity of the islanders.

Paula said perceptively, 'You didn't like him.'

Cressida smiled with irony. 'I don't like people who gloat. It gave him a real kick to live in absolute luxury while half a mile away men lived knowing that if they didn't catch fish that day there would be no protein for their children.'

'That's depraved!'

Cressida shrugged, avoiding any comment on that. 'He'd been poor, too. I suppose it was his way of reinforcing his security.'

'Was he pleased to see you?' asked Paula.

Very pleased. His latest mistress had just left in high dudgeon and he was bored with life by himself. The island girls, who had a much more wholesome attitude to sex than he did, were altogether too matter-of-fact about it to satisfy him. He had frightened Cressida.

She said noncomittally, 'I think he was bored, yes, but we weren't there for long. We had dinner with him and left the next day.'

Paula said, 'And was that all?'

Cressida was startled. She looked up sharply to discover that they were all watching her. Something in her voice must have given her away. She managed to smile and say lightly, 'Yes, that's all, except that that's where I tasted *foie gras* for the only time in my life.'

'Didn't you like it?' Mrs Scrivener sounded comfortably shocked at the idea of having one of the delights of French cuisine on an island in the Pacific.

'I loved it,' Cressida told her shortly. 'But when I realised what it was, and how it's made, I'm afraid it made me feel a little ill.'

That started off a discussion on the merits of vegetarianism, which proceeded with the amiable acrimony of old friends. Cressida leaned back, glad that the spotlight was lifted. She had been lying, of course. The millionaire had wanted her to stay; his greedy eyes had somehow discerned her innocence and, like a child who can only enjoy what he despoils, he had wanted to replace that innocence with knowledge, introduce her to degradation. It had come as a shock to him to realise that she was not for the taking; her mouth tightened as she remembered how he had tried to buy her from her father, tempting him with all sorts of inducements, even offering to supply a crew for the yacht until he became bored with her.

It had been an appalling scene. Her father had gone icy with revulsion and they had left the opulent air-conditioned house with its decadent décor and stuffy atmosphere, and gone out into the tropical night to the sound of the astonished owner wondering why they didn't grasp their opportunities with both hands.

He had come down to see them off the next day, still obviously a little dumbfounded at their intransigence.

His favourite comment, Cressida remembered, had been, 'But that's Victorian! People don't act that way now. This is the twentieth century!'

A little shiver pulled her skin tight. She wriggled slightly, but the feeling of unease persisted. At last she looked from beneath her lashes to where Luke sat, his half-closed eyes gleaming as they scanned her face. The flames of the fire were a flickering light, picking out the stark contours of his face with loving exactness. He was relaxed in a big armchair, one hand lying along the upholstered arm in a pose which epitomised his complete control of his surroundings, yet she sensed an errant wildness beneath the indolent posture, something untamed and fierce beating up through the control he used as a barrier.

And deep within herself an answering wildness responded, so that for a second she fancied she understood what lay hidden, coiled in the furthermost parts of his complex character.

Her eyes glittered like jewels; her expression altered so infinitesimally that she was unaware of it, but from her face a woman looked out, alive with woman's knowledge, taunting and aware and boldly sensual, aflame with a promise which was as basic to the human race as the desire for security.

Luke's expression froze, and Cressida cringed back into her chair, turning her face abruptly away so that he couldn't read in it whatever had brought that icy change to his expression. Oh, you fool, she castigated herself, he saw, he knows!

For the rest of the evening she was content to let Paula monopolise the conversation; she answered when she was spoken to, but apart from that volunteered little, and she went early up to bed.

It was only the tiredness of her healthy young body which brought her sleep that night, and only a grittily determined strength she hadn't known she possessed that helped her through the weekend, because it dragged mercilessly. Somehow, Paula had discerned a little of what had happened so quickly and so silently in front of the fire, for when she spoke to Cressida again it was with a hint of reserve. She was no less pleasant, just as charming, but there was a touch of frost in her eyes which hurt Cressida at the same time as it made her feel a wicked and most rebellious defiance.

She was glad when Luke took Paula back late on Sunday; she even hoped he would stay the night in Auckland, although the thought of them together, lovers in a big bed, tore at her brain and heart. To make sure that she didn't meet him again that night, she made up a headache and went up to her room.

And there she relived the incident she had interrupted after lunch that day, relived it with torment and tears, because she knew now that any little hidden hopes she might have had were doomed.

Over lunch Luke had mentioned that he had given permission for a university team to excavate a series of gardens around the foot of one of the *pa* sites, and the resulting conversation had decided Cressida to learn something of Maori explorers and pioneers of a thousand years ago. She had gone to the library, intent on getting a copy of a popular anthropological work about New Zealand's Maori discoverers. The room was big and dim, and she had crouched down behind a large leather sofa to examine a promising row of books when the door opened and Paula's voice froze her.

'. . . the wrong weekend!' she was saying, half laughing, half complaining. The door slammed and before Cressida could climb to her feet Paula's voice came again, but now it had altered, thickened and intimate with undertones which held Cressida frozen.

'Oh God, darling! I need you so much—sometimes I think I'm going mad. What on earth am I to do?'

After that there was the kind of silence that throbs, and reluctantly, anguished, Cressida forced herself to stay still, holding her hands over her ears to block out the sound of their voices when they began to speak again.

Cressida clamped her eyes shut, ground the heels of her hands into her ears and wondered through the roaring this caused how she had managed to get herself in this position. But through the embarrassment and the humiliation and the fear that she might be discovered was pain, pure and simple, sharp as a sword and as clean as crystal, and she felt as though her soul was shattering into pieces.

At long last a silence persuaded her that she had been left alone, surely the most reluctant eavesdropper in the world. Slowly, carefully, she eased the pressure of her hands, opened her eyes a slit. Outside, a spring shower hurtled across the sky, sending cold fresh rain on to the garden, and darkening the room to dusk. A distant roll of thunder muttered sulkily around the horizon, then a blackbird began to sing, clear and brilliant in the sudden silence.

Cressida began to breathe again. Cautiously she eased her stiff body away from its huddle by the shelves.

And then Paula moaned, shockingly loud in the stillness. 'Oh God, darling, God, darling, please . . .'

Cressida's heart slammed still, then began to beat again in a rapid threatened motion. Her eyes swung to where they stood; before she closed them again what she saw was burned into her brain. Paula, dwarfed by Luke's presence, her face lifted in rapture and a strange driven hunger sharpening the exquisite features. Her arms were locked about his neck, her long fingernails pressed into the dark chestnut hair. Luke's face was hidden, but his arms were bars across her slender back and she was melded against him from breast to knee, exquisitely fragile against the raw power of his body.

Cressida froze; she didn't hear Luke's deep reply, but she registered when they left the room shortly after. For another half-hour she stayed, huddled and racked with shivers, and when she left it was by the french doors out on to the lawn. She felt smirched and dirty, as though she had done something shameful.

When she died, that image would still be imprinted on her retinas: the open hunger in Paula's face taunting her, the lazy intimacy of Luke's tone tearing the frail wisps of her unexpressed dreams into tatters.

That afternoon she walked and walked across the

vivid grass to the base of one of the cliffs, trying to find some sort of reason and logic in her situation. Hands in her pockets, because the air was crisp and keen even though the sun shone, she strode with hunched shoulders and eyes fixed on the ground, occasionally stopping to look about her with blind eyes that saw little of the countryside.

She came to some conclusions, bleak and comfortless enough, but they gave her some peace of mind. It was, she found, simple enough to view things with a degree of sanity if she assumed that there were really two situations with very little in common. One was the fact that Luke and Paula were in love; it hurt, but it had nothing to do with her. She was, as she had been all her life, the outsider.

The other, her situation, was painful too, but at least she had a role of some dignity in it. She was violently physically attracted to a man she barely knew. It would, in time, pass, but until it did she would suffer this anguish. First love had to happen to everyone; how she looked back on it in later years would depend on her, because she knew enough of Luke by now to understand that, although he would not give her false hopes, he would treat her and her poor little bruised heart with courtesy and consideration.

And if they seemed wishy-washy qualities compared to the burning need for satisfaction which had roughened Paula's voice and flamed from her face—well, Cressida had only to recall that millionaire who had wanted to buy the use of her body from her father to realise that she could have fallen in love with a man who was less than considerate.

It was easy enough to arrive at conclusions when she was free of the snare Luke had set unwittingly

about her heart and mind, not quite so simple to
follow them through when she arrived back at the
homestead and was met by a Luke who looked far
from pleased with her.

'In future,' he said coldly as she wrenched her
gumboots off, 'tell someone where you plan to go, and
how long you plan to be away.'

Cressida stared at him, her expression astounded.
'Why? I will, of course, but what on earth could
happen to me here?'

'Plenty. The creeks are in flood, there are some
extremely short-tempered bulls lurking about, and no
place is entirely safe.'

She bristled, but the green-gold smoulder of his eyes
stopped the quick smart reply which came unbidden
to her lips, and after a moment Luke finished more
mildly, 'Mother was a little concerned.'

'I'm sorry,' she said quickly. 'I'll go and tell her I'm
back.'

'No hurry.' He reached out to smooth a damp
strand of hair back from her wind-cooled cheek, and
said firmly, 'We saw your long legs pacing around the
hills about ten minutes ago, so she's not worried now.
Go and dry yourself off.'

Her breath caught in her throat, but she managed to
move away from his touch without betraying just how
powerfully it affected her. She swallowed, remembering how he had held Paula, and the bleakness of
that moment froze the muscles in her face, chilling
her expression.

'What is it?' asked Luke.

He saw too much. She shivered and replied, 'I'm
cold.'

An ironic eyebrow lifted as his eyes moved from her
face to the parka she still had on. However, although

he must have known she was evading him, he said nothing more, merely waiting while she pulled it off and hung it up, then followed her through the door that led into the house proper.

The rest of the afternoon had been uncomfortable; with an awareness sharpened by her obsession, Cressida realised that something was wrong. Paula was all sharp edges, donning a glittering, brittle mask over her emotions. Luke looked—drained, as if something had happened that had hurt him.

And he had come home just after dark, only a few minutes after Cressida had fled up to her room. Now, hours later, she watched as the stars came out, bold and flaunting in the clear sky. She knew them all, the lovely southern constellations as well as the familiar stars of the zodiac; out of sight beyond the horizon were the ones that shone down from the skies of the northern hemisphere. She knew them all, yet could call none of them hers. Years ago, she had read the legend of the Flying Dutchman, doomed to wander the seas down the centuries until redeemed by the love of a woman. Sometimes she felt like him, a wanderer with no place to call her own, no one to love.

The eternal outsider, the child with its face pressed up against the windowpane, greedily watching a scene it knew could never be its own.

And self-pity, she told herself robustly as she turned away from contemplation of those beautiful, implacable stars, had to be the most debilitating of emotions. She would not succumb to it.

For the next week or so, Luke worked like a galley slave out on the station, as though by exhausting himself he could find relief from the emotions that were tearing at him. Cressida wanted so much to ease the pain that she glimpsed behind the smooth mask he turned to the rest of the world, that she too seemed to be driven by devils. She spent hours in her room, practising on the typewriter Luke had brought home for her from Auckland. Fortunately, she discovered that either she had a talent for it or hard work made it easier; Marie praised her lavishly and she responded with even more effort.

Then, one night, as she was reading beside the fire, Luke came through the door. Cressida loked up and met his eyes, felt the beginnings of a blush and managed to short-circuit it by hastily rearranging her legs so that she was no longer sprawled out along the sofa.

'I think your mother is in the kitchen, making marmalade,' she offered.

He grinned. 'I have no doubt of it—the smell permeates the house! But as it happens, it's you I want. Would you like to come to Whangarei with me tomorrow?'

'Yes,' she said simply, adding shyly, 'Why are we going?'

'A day out?' He watched her from hodded eyes, nothing but a slightly taunting expression on his face. 'I have some business to attend to, and there's a display in the community centre of that group of artists you were talking about yesterday.'

Cressida was surprised and showed it, because when she and Mrs Scrivener had been discussing the review of the exhibition Luke had been immersed in a mass of papers.

He laughed and said, 'I have good ears. Well, how about it?'

'I'd love to go,' she said, her spirits soaring. Pleasure irradiated her expression and the smile she gave him was warmly expectant.

His mouth tightened, and the smile faded. 'Luke?' she ventured.

He said wryly, 'I keep forgetting how young you are.'

'Is enthusiasm a sign of extreme youth?'

The words were snapped out like bullets, and he laughed softly, something hard appearing in the depths of his eyes. 'It can be.'

Cressida had to hold herself still as he came towards her, because his smooth walk registered as danger on her personal scale; her eyes dilated, then fluttered closed as he pulled her to her feet.

'This,' he said deliberately, hateful amusement colouring his tones, 'is what reveals your youth, my dear girl.'

His fingers slid up her arms; she stood stiffly, waiting for she knew not what, and flinched as a knowing hand came to rest on the pulse that fluttered at the base of her throat.

Her eyelids were heavy, weighed down by sensation. From beneath her lashes she risked a slanting glance at him and saw the cold ruthlessness that carved his features. Strange shivering sensations plucked at her nerves, burned through tissue and skin into her very core. Heat from his body enclosed her like a cloak, yet she shivered, mouth and lips suddenly dry. She had to touch her tongue to her top lip; Luke saw the tiny movement and his eyes flicked from their fascination with the long pale line of her throat to her face.

Instantly a shutter fell, closing off the vitality and awareness which had blazed so short a time in his expression. His eyes turned green, cold and sharp as emerald splinters. Cressida's face was stiff with shame and hurt. She tried to pull away, and when he wouldn't

102 THE SWEETEST TRAP

let her go, holding her still with an imperative hand on her upper arm, she turned her head away, letting her lashes droop down over her eyes so that he couldn't see behind them.

He said with an insistence which was gentle yet merciless, 'Tell me about the millionaire you met on that island.'

If he had wanted to shock her, he succeeded. Her eyes flew open and she shrank even further away as her throat closed up. Dumbly, she shook her head.

'Tell me,' he repeated, adding after a moment, 'Did he make a pass at you, Cressida?'

Colour scorched through her, then receded, leaving her pale and shaking. Her father had never referred to the incident, banishing it as though it had never happened, and she had been so shocked that she had preferred not to think of it.

Some impulsive reaction had persuaded her to drag it up from her subconscious. Perhaps she had wanted to remember that someone had found her attractive; Paula was a lot of competition. Since that night, she had pushed the memory of it back into the dark recesses of her mind. Even to think of it made her sick.

Huskily, because her throat was tight and painful, she said, 'It wasn't anything. I just didn't like the man.'

'You're sickened by the memory,' Luke corrected implacably. 'What really happened, Cressida?'

In an agony of indecision, she bit her lip. He watched her, his fingers on her arm relaxing but forming a manacle stronger than iron. She wilted at the power of the will emanating from him, controlled yet utterly ruthless, and when she whispered, 'All right,' it was a surrender.

In a bleak little voice she told him about the man and his desire for her, careful not to look his way as the painful words came with difficulty to her tongue.

Towards the end her voice faltered, became so soft that he had to strain to hear it, but she finished on a hard, defiant note, 'And that was all there was to it. He just wanted someone to entertain him for a few weeks, and I was the nearest.'

'What made you remember the incident the other night? From your reluctance to discuss it, I gather you think about it as rarely as possible.'

Cressida's shoulder lifted in the smallest of shrugs. Because she suspected the answer was not flattering to her, she said in a gruff, offhand voice, 'I don't know. Why do you want to know?'

The hand keeping her prisoner tightened, then the long fingers relaxed and fell away. Luke said quietly, 'Because the distaste and fear in your eyes is an abomination. No woman should ever feel that way.'

She shrugged again. 'It happens. Although *nothing* really happened.'

'Few men take a salacious pleasure in the destruction of inocence, Cressida. He wanted to introduce you to degradation because he was bored with women experienced enough to know him for what he was. The initiation of a virgin would have been a tasty morsel for his kind of dissipated appetite. Men like him are rare, as you'll find out.'

She looked at him with something like pleading, her face very young and vulnerable. 'I thought it might be—I thought he could see something in me that he recognised,' she muttered, flushing yet determined, because until then she had refused to admit this fear even to herself.

Luke said something short and blistering, then hugged her to him, lending her the comfort of his big body in an embrace that was pure compassion.

'How could he see anything in you when he was so blind? You're not responsible for the way men look at you, Cressida. I don't think I've ever met a woman who's less aware of her own attractions.' He held her away from him, transfixing her with his gaze. 'Remember that. Self-respect is all that matters. No one can take that away from you without your active co-operation.'

She nodded, seeing kindness in his eyes, in his face, and with the kindness a severity which underpinned it and emphasised it. Cressida recalled his bedroom, austere yet opulent, and thought Luke would be harder on himself than on anyone else. In him, recklessness warred with a fastidious restraint; he was a complex man, and she had no hope of understanding him.

She smiled and said simply, 'Thank you.'

His answering smile gleamed with amusement and something else, a kind of wry derision which she felt was directed at himself. 'Think nothing of it,' he said lightly. 'My sister tells me on occasion that I have a talent for being a brother.'

Well, if he liked to think that was how she saw him, she could only fall in with it. She stood on tiptoes and kissed his cheek just below the strong bone, saying demurely as she stepped away, 'Bossy, yes, but I'd agree.'

Luke laughed shortly and looked up as Mrs Scrivener came into the room to tell them that her marmalade had set beautifully and did they want a cup of tea?

For the rest of the evening Cressida hugged her memories of those precious few minutes to herself, aware that they might have to last her a lifetime, and when she went up to her room it was to drift around it for an hour or so before she could summon up the resolution to go to bed.

CHAPTER FIVE

ONCE Cressida had got into bed, it took her a long time to get to sleep. For hours she lay quietly, recalling Luke's unexpected kindness and the understanding which had taken the sting from the memory. She found herself wondering why her father hadn't realised that she needed to be reassured; surely he must have seen that the sordid incident had left her shamed and afraid?

If he had, apparently he had considered it neither necessary nor important to dispel her fears.

But Luke had understood. Although he was autocratic and dominating, very much in control of his world, she should not make the mistake of putting him in the same category as her father.

Luke, she thought, smiling, was different in a very important way.

She woke late and had to hurry to dress so that she didn't keep him waiting. When she came downstairs, it was to discover that he had already had breakfast but was still drinking coffee over at the window, his long body lounging negligently against the wall. Acutely conscious of his scrutiny, Cressida responded to his greeting with a cautious smile before applying herself to toast. Like many other people she was discovering that confession might be good for the soul, but it made for embarrassing mornings after.

After a moment, Luke turned his regard back to the window and she allowed her eyes to wander across the room. So big a man should not be graceful, yet there was the powerful elegance of a wild animal in his stance and movements. He possessed the vitality of perfect health, the easy posture of the very fit, and underlying it all was a smouldering sexuality which was stronger for being uncontrived.

Cressida could understand why Paula Radford's face had worn that expression of agonised ecstasy, why she was unable to give him up even though their lives could never mesh. But she thought Paula was a fool.

If he loved me, she thought wistfully, I would give up everything for him.

The realisation of what she had just said in her mind made her jaw clench suddenly on the remnants of the toast.

That must have been the way her mother had felt about her father, and look where it had got her! Cressida chewed carefully and swallowed with a dry throat. How she wished her mother was still alive to tell her whether her wholesale surrender of her life had been worthwhile.

Comforted by Luke's kindness, she had been in danger of forgetting that love was the biggest prison of all. It would pay, she decided with a stern resolve, never to lose sight of it again.

'That,' he observed mildly, 'is a fairly fierce look you're bestowing on the toast rack. What did it do to you?'

She smiled, a hint of recklessness showing through. 'Nothing. Are you ready to go?'

'Give me five minutes.' He paced across to the table and set his cup and saucer down before holding the chair out as she got to her feet.

She kept her head high and her face impassive as he examined her, but it was difficult to breathe when he touched her cheek with a gentle finger and asked, 'Everything all right?'

Cressida nodded, colouring faintly. 'Yes, thank you.'

Laughter lit up the depths of his hard eyes. 'Good. I'll see you at the door in five minutes.'

Cressida ran up the stairs to her room, grabbed her bag and fled down again, arriving just as the Land Rover arrived on the gravel outside. In the front beside Luke was Marie's husband; he smiled at her and hurried out to open the door. A little taken aback, because she hadn't expected to fly down to Whangarei, Cressida climbed in and sat primly between the two men as they set off through the green and gold morning for the airstrip.

While she waited beside the plane for Luke to make the checks, she watched mynahs strut in their jerky fashion across the paddock, exactly as if they were picking their way across shards of glass. Sinister as bandits with their black masks and yellow eyes and beaks, they were arrogant and dominating, chasing away the sparrows that moved across the airstrip in small bobbing groups.

'Ready?'

At Luke's question she assented and was helped up into the cockpit, her legs showing smooth and brown and unstockinged beneath the denim skirt she wore. She had flown very little and never in a plane as small as the Cessna, so she almost held her breath while he went through the procedure of starting the engines.

He must have been able to sense her unease, for without turning his head he dropped a hand over her tense ones, squeezing them for a moment. 'You don't need to be nervous. I'm a very cautious pilot.'

The fleeting recklessness that spiced his grin gave the lie to his observation, but it vanished the moment the engine roared into life. Then he was all concentration. And soon Cressida discovered that she wasn't nervous, indeed, that she enjoyed flying. As the ground fell away beneath them and the plane steadied and all the splendour of land and sea gleamed like a magical chart beneath them, she exhaled on a long sigh and breathed, 'This must be the most beautiful country in the world.'

'I've yet to find a lovelier.'

That was all Luke said, but she could hear his love for his homeland reverberate in his voice, and she was seized by a pang of envy so great that it was almost physical, a pain in the region of her heart.

Shyly she asked, 'Do you think an outsider can ever feel about a country as—well, as you do?'

'Of course, plenty of people have. Everyone in New Zealand is descended from immigrants, you know. Didn't your mother tell you about her homeland?'

'Sometimes, although my father didn't like to hear her talking about it. I think he resented the fact that she was sometimes homesick. She came from Westland in the South Island, and she used to tell me tall tales about the life there.'

He laughed. 'They probably weren't tall tales at all. Westland is a place on its own, and they have their own customs and habits and character, as we do here in Northland. We're different, we have a different history. Most of the Dalmatians who arrived from Yugoslavia at the end of last century and the beginning of this came to dig kauri gum on the gumfields of Northland. The gum has gone, but they stayed and became farmers and set up our wine industry. They help give Northland its unique flavour.'

He began to point out places of interest below them, taking them over Kerikeri so that she could see the orchards around the little town, with their rows of kiwi-fruit vines between high hedges, and the darker green globes which were citrus trees. Beyond Kerikeri was the Bay of Islands, glittering and beckoning from every one of its many long inlets, the islands scattered and green across the placid sea.

After that there were rugged hills covered in the forest which Cressida was learning to call the bush, a hundred shades of green with the Catherine wheels of ponga ferns exploding wherever there was a gap in the canopy, and drifts of the purest white which Luke told her were the flowers of the native clematis. On both sides of the peninsula which was Northland, as far as she could see was the gleaming silver sheet of the sea, to the west the dangerously turbulent Tasman, to the east the inaptly named Pacific Ocean, home of tropical islands and coconuts and volcanoes and immense hurricanes far to the north.

'It looks like the map of an enchanted country,' she said as they swooped in over the little city of Whangarei, set between the harbour and the hills, some of them volcanoes from a violent and unimaginable past.

'You're a romantic.'

Cressida shook her head, her mouth curling a slow smile. 'I said it looked like an enchanted country, not that it is one. I don't think I'm very romantic.'

'You should be. Everyone is entitled to one year of unbridled romanticism, usually the one from nineteen to twenty. Otherwise it bursts through later in life and creates the very devil.'

There was an odd note in Luke's voice which caught her attention. She looked over and surprised a grim twist to his mouth, but a moment later it was gone, leaving her to wonder uncomfortably if he was recalling an affair with a married woman long ago, and its aftermath.

A hired car waited for them at the small airport, its keys handed over by a woman whose expression made it clear that she admired the tall man with bronze hair who smiled at her with such unbidden charm. Cressida discovered that it was possible to feel smug and jealous at the same time; she hated the uncomfortable sensation and was rather abrupt as they drove the short distance from Onerahi to the city centre, past the town basin where the overseas yachts were tied up. Cressida surveyed them with a knowledgeable eye, but felt not a whit of envy.

After he had switched off the engine in the car park of a substantial building, Luke turned to her. 'I'll be spending at least two hours in here. I'll get one of the office girls to take you into town—it's about five minutes' walk to the main shopping street.'

'I can take myself,' she said a little indignantly, adding, 'I'm not a complete novice at getting around strange towns, you know.'

He grinned and undid his seat-belt. 'I wonder where I got the idea that your father kept pretty close tabs on you!'

Honesty forced her to concede that. 'But only until we knew whether a place was safe or not.'

'I doubt if you'd find any place much safer than Whangarei. But you don't want me to worry all through this directors' meeting, do you?'

He was laughing at her, but when his eyes gleamed with amusement and an almost tender mischief like that she could refuse him nothing.

Susie Flagg, who was relieved of her duties as a typist to act as escort, was a year or so older than Cressida, cheerful and friendly and brisk. 'Where do you want to go?' she asked. Another woman visibly impressed by Luke.

He said smoothly, 'She wants to buy some clothes.' A flashing smile, and Susie fluttered. 'You look as though you can tell her the best places to shop.'

The implied compliment brought bemused colour to

Susie's cheeks. 'Thank you,' she managed. 'I love shopping, and there are quite a few good places here.'

Hovering in the background was the middle-aged executive who had chosen Susie without any sign of protest at having her relieved of her work. Clearly anxious to hurry Luke away, he was not confident enough to state his impatience. Cressida could almost see his sigh of relief as Luke turned towards him. The older man began to usher him towards the lift.

'I'll just go and get my bag,' Susie told her. 'Do you mind waiting here?'

'No, not at all.'

Cressida heard the ting of the lift bell; it took her a considerable amount of courage not to gaze after Luke as though he were her one hope of salvation. Composing her face, she tried for a cheerful insouciant smile, only to see him say something to the man he was with and stride back across the foyer towards her.

'How much money have you got?'

She gaped, and he went on impatiently, 'Come on, Cressida, this is no time to cavil. You'll need, at the very least, a couple of hundred dollars. Have you got that much?'

'Yes.' The lawyer had sent her five hundred dollars, but she wasn't going to spend it all on clothes, not even two hundred of it! It could well be very necessary later on, when she had outworn her welcome at Five Mile.

Luke surveyed her with narrowed eyes, as though he suspected her of lying, then gave a short nod. 'Very well, then. I'll see you in a couple of hours' time.'

On his way back to the by now very impatient executive, he met Susie; he stopped and gave her a few brief orders, finishing with the dazzling smile he used so carelessly, and laughed at her response before going on his way.

Susie was still smiling as she came up to Cressida. 'Oh lord, he's gorgeous, isn't he? My heart hasn't had such a workout for years!'

She was fun, and she certainly enjoyed shopping. She was good at it too, thrifty and careful, with an eye to quality and cut. At first, knowing herself to be entirely inexperienced in the buying of clothes for pleasure, Cressida left the decisions to her companion, but Susie wasn't satisfied with that.

'You have to wear them,' she said a little severely. 'You have to decide if you feel good in them and if you like the way you look in them, otherwise you might just as well get a saleswoman to choose them. You're lucky, you've got those slender bones and long legs, anything will look good on you, but you need to feel that they're right for you.'

Cressida nodded; Susie looked so good herself, she clearly knew what she was talking about. But not all the other girl's persuasion could coax Cressida into buying any more than some very necessary underwear and two cotton dresses and a pair of sandals, and she was appalled at how short a distance her money went. After a keen glance at Cressida's set expression, Susie said cheerfully, 'Right, you can treat this as a learning experience, if you like. It doesn't cost anything to try clothes on.'

'It hardly seems fair if I'm not intending to buy anything,' Cressida objected.

'Nonsense, any dress shop worth its salt is eager to persuade you into their clothes. You might not buy today, but who knows about tomorrow?'

This was unanswerable, so Cressida allowed herself to be swathed in clothes ranging from exquisite evening dresses in an exclusive little boutique to casual but well-made cottons, and the frankly fun outfits in the chain stores. Nor did it stop at clothes. There were shoes and bathing suits, bags and belts and scarves, even a range of make-up which had Susie and the saleswoman happily trying on colour after colour before choosing the perfect cosmetics for her tanned skin.

At last, exhausted and hot because the lovely fresh morning had turned into a blazing day, Cressida called a halt. She and Susie walked back beneath wide verandas that shaded the sultry footpaths, and there, just inside the foyer, was Luke, tall and somehow much more positive-looking than the men who were gathered around him.

He looked up as they came in through the door, said something and detached himself from the group, coming towards them with the smooth stride of an athlete.

Cressida felt her mouth dry; she smiled a little uncertainly as his eyes went from her face to the few parcels she had in her hand, and narrowed for a few seconds.

'You need to comb your hair,' he said lightly, touching a black tress which was lying damply against the nape of her neck.

'I'll take you to the cloakroom.' Susie was eager to help.

Luke nodded and stretched out a lean brown hand for the parcels. 'Thank you. When you've shown Cressida where it is, can I see you back here?'

Suspicion stirred in Cressida's mind. She looked up sharply, to be met by the blandest green gaze she had ever seen. After a moment of mental struggle, she chided herself for being so paranoid and meekly followed her companion to the cloakroom.

Whatever he had to say to Susie was brief, because when Cressida emerged after combing her hair and washing her face he was alone, the cynosure of all eyes in the foyer. And although he had to be aware of his effect on his fellow humans there was no sign of conceit or self-consciousness in him, only the natural arrogance of a man who is completely in command of himself and his life.

He took Cressida to lunch in a pleasant restaurant with tables in a leafy courtyard and the kind of superb cuisine she was realising was a New Zealand speciality, magnificently fresh ingredients cooked plainly but well. With an appetite which started out languid but sharpened almost immediately, she ate fish fillets with a mussel sauce and a salad which seemed to have been picked a few minutes before.

Luke refused wine, ordering mineral water with the comment, 'I don't drink when I'm flying, but if you want some, they do a pleasant house white . . .?'

'No, mineral water will be lovely, thank you.'

It was, too, cold and faintly bubbly, with a hint of lemon in it. It went perfectly with her meal, even with the kiwi-fruit concoction both she and Luke chose to follow, a fluffy meld of meringue and whipped cream, dramatised by the green and black slices of the berries.

'Oh dear,' she sighed when it had all gone. 'Bliss! I love kiwi-fruit.'

'We get given them by the ton in the season,' he said a little sardonically. He laughed at her startled look and explained, 'Friends in Kerikeri produce them for the export market. The standards are incredibly high, every fruit not only has to look perfect, it has to be the right size and shape. The rejects are far too many to be absorbed by the home market, so they get dumped as cattle food, pig food, used as mulch for the vines, or just given away. Our beasts enjoy them immensely as a change from grass.'

'It seems a sin,' mourned Cressida. Then she laughed.

'I'll bet New Zealand's the only place in the world where cattle get fed on luxury food!'

'Oh, not at all. The best beef in Japan is fed on beer and massaged to achieve the perfect blend of fat and meat.'

She pulled a face at that, but conceded that if the animals had to be killed they might just as well be happy while they were alive. Pleasure curled in lazy streams through her body and mind, seducing her. It was wonderful to be sitting with Luke in this pretty courtyard, among azaleas in tubs, watching the play of expression over the hard clever face, enjoying conversation which was entirely free from any taint of patronage.

When she was with him he managed to make her feel that she was the only woman of any importance in his life. A cynical little part of her mind observed that it was probably a very useful knack, and no doubt worked well with all women, but she thrust it to the back of her head. She was going to enjoy this day, this time with him. She was sick of being sensible and cautious. A delicious recklessness gleamed in her eyes, gave a richer curve to her mouth.

After all, she reasoned, succumbing to it couldn't get her into any trouble. Luke was in love with Paula Radford. And although she suspected that he found his temporary guest attractive, he was too controlled to give in to what was only a physical attraction.

So she allowed her instincts to take over, not realising how provocative they made her as she brought a delicately teasing innocence to the art of flirtation.

Luke gave no sign that he was taken aback. He responded with a polished worldliness, understated and spiced with mockery, which sent her heart-rate up through the ceiling. She discovered the subtle pleasure of flirting with an exciting man, and for a few minutes forgot that he represented a far greater danger to her than the decadent millionaire who had lusted to take her innocence. For she could fall in love with Luke, whereas that other man would have been unable to touch the essential Cressida.

At last he said, with a wry smile which made fun of his own reluctance, 'It's a long time since I've allowed myself to be beguiled by a pretty woman into sitting in the sun and flirting. Delightful though it's been, we'd better get going.'

On an impulse, she said quickly, before she had time to think better of it, 'Thank you.'

He held the chair for her as she got to her feet. 'Whatever for?'

'For a lovely day.'

She thought she detected a hint of compassion in his tones as he said, 'You're easily pleased, Cressida.'

She didn't want him to feel sorry for her, so she flashed him a mischievous smile. 'I have simple tastes.'

He took her arm and led her out on to the heat of the pavement, saying with open amusement, 'With very little encouragement, you could develop into a minx. We'd better get home.'

The Cessna was waiting for them at the airport, sleek and ready to go. Cressida waited while Luke handed back the car keys, then watched without understanding as a porter came over and began to unload a pile of parcels from the boot. She was incurious until she caught sight of a name on one of them. It was that of the very expensive little boutique where Susie had persuaded her into such pretty party dresses. Perhaps Luke had collected a parcel for his mother . . .

The suspicion she had managed to quell before came raging back. She followed the porter numbly out to where the plane waited and stood stiff and furious beside it. The porter unloaded the parcels into the plane, accepted her thanks with a shy smile and walked off. Almost immediately, Luke came out of the terminus building. From high overhead a nesting lark poured out his pride of territory, the crystalline trills and cascades of notes piercing, shrilly sublime in the warm air.

With eyes which were almost black with emotion, Cressida watched the man walk towards her, saw the sun gleam bronze and russet in his hair, the long easy stride which made him so immediately distinguishable, the smooth flection and contraction of the muscles in his thighs. And the harshly hewn features, alight with a sardonic challenge as he smiled down at her.

'In you get,' he said.

She asked flatly, 'Are those parcels for your mother?'

'No. They're for you. Are you going to get in, or shall I pick you up and throw you in?'

She was so angry that it was difficult to pronounce the words. 'I can't afford——'

'Consider it a loan,' he interrupted, boredom chilling his voice. He gripped her shoulder, turning her towards the plane.

Angrily Cressida hunched away, and felt his hand tighten. 'I don't want to spend vast amounts on myself,' she protested, half sobbing with frustration. 'I don't know how much there is for me, and I'll have to keep myself until I've trained for a job. I——'

He jerked her around to face him, his face set into harshly angular lines. 'For heaven's sake, Cressida, we won't let your starve! Have you been worrying all this time about your future?'

Her eyes drowned as she looked up at him. 'I have to,' she explained thickly. 'I've only got myself, Luke—and I don't want your pity!'

'I don't pity graceless, undisciplined adolescents,' he returned grimly. 'Get into the plane.'

Cressida obeyed, because like that he was frightening, his mouth tight and controlled, the words delivered with a cutting emphasis that slashed her fragile composure to ribbons. Too tense to be able to choose her words carefully, she huddled into the seat, staring out with miserable, unseeing eyes as Luke went about getting them into the air.

In fact, neither of them spoke until they were almost half-way home. Then he said in an uncompromising voice, 'I want your promise that you won't upset my mother. This is between you and me.' And, when she didn't immediately give him the assurance he sought, he shot her a hard level stare and continued, 'Have I your word?'

'I—yes, I suppose so. But Luke, I can't take those clothes. I saw the prices on them, I know how much they cost. Even if—even if I have enough money, I won't be living the sort of life where I'll need clothes like that.'

'Why? Most women of your age have a wardrobe built up over the years. Because of the exigencies of your life you haven't. You're not planning to live like a hermit, I trust?'

The lick of sarcasm in his voice made her retreat into a miserable defiance. 'No,' she said in muted tones, hating herself for the weakness which made her so susceptible to intimidation. 'No, but I didn't plan to go to parties much, either. Not formal ones, anyway.'

'Why not? If you go to Auckland, you'll be asked out frequently. We have relatives, a lot of friends there.' The question was put in a detached, academic tone, but at her silence his voice hardened and he asked, 'Or were you planning to cut all ties with us, Cressida?'

Since she had been planning to do just that, she knew

that she looked guilty. She said almost pleadingly, 'I can't just—just move in on your life.'

But what she meant was, I can't let you take over my life.

Luke knew that she was being evasive. A brow lifted and he said neutrally, 'I thought you liked us.'

'I do.' Her resolution stiffened. She recognised these tactics. 'Very much, as you're well aware. But it would be rank presumption if I expected you to provide me with a social circle as well as all the kindness you've shown me.'

'If you expected it, yes, but you don't. We like you, in a way, we're the only family you have. I'd like to know that you feel you can depend on us.'

Fair words, so she nodded, because how could she say that she wanted to get away from him, she was afraid that she was falling in love with him and she could only be hurt by it?

She said gruffly, 'Of course,' and directed a reluctant glance his way.

His profile was stark against the glowing mellow blue of the sky, an incisive outline of angles, indicative of power and strength. He was a possessive man, the instincts buried deep but always there. He had grown up knowing that his heritage was secure, that in time he would rule over his kingdom, and he knew that he could do it, he had a bone-deep confidence which nothing would ever shake. And, because she had arrived on his doorstep, because he had rescued her, he had incorporated her into his other responsibilities and was angry that she showed signs of rebellion.

He did not realise how arrogant he was, she thought, half resentful, half envious.

Then he turned his head to meet her reluctant gaze and although his eyes were still stormy there was sympathy there too.

'Humour me,' he said blandly, shocking her with his astuteness. 'I've been constantly accused of being the most domineering man alive but, although I accept that there's a measure of truth in it, I'm not a dictator. I only want you to be happy.'

Yes, she could accept that. Her mouth curved. 'Your sister?'

A grin brought her laughter, husky and tantalising, in the narrow confines of the cabin. Luke's lashes drooped to half cover his eyes, but he said merely, 'Yes, my sister. She worked her way through the thesaurus finding words to describe me. Helped her vocabulary no end.'

All Cressida's amusement could not banish the cold recognition at the back of her brain. He was as much a dictator as her father, only much more dangerous because she was so susceptible to him. He might have met his match in Paula Radford; love was the wild card in the pack, but he had no hesitation in persuading others—or forcing them—to do his will.

Perhaps it was then, the boxes of clothes behind her invisible but very much felt, that she began to make plans to leave. Five Mile, with all its attractions, could turn out to be as much a prison as the *Windhover* had been.

Later that evening in her room, she attacked the boxes, wondering which clothes Susie had decided to buy for her. With hindsight, it was easy enough to see how Luke had managed it. No doubt Susie had organised the sale and packing of the clothes while Cressida had been in the changing-rooms in each place. And presumably Luke's name was enough to guarantee payment.

Distastefully she unpacked two evening dresses, a variety of dresses and frivolous underwear, bathing suits and shoes, even the cosmetics. Her brows met as she found a flask of perfume—*Ivoire*, fresh and floral, with a sensual base. What had made Susie choose that particular scent? Absently she touched the stem to her wrists and sniffed, her expression dreamy. It was beautiful.

Mrs Scrivener had said that there were to be guests at dinner, two men who were doing an archaeological survey of that area, so Cressida took down one of the dresses which Susie had chosen, a fine jersey in a subtle princess line which gave her the look of a sophisticated schoolgirl. The pink colour warmed her fading tan so that she needed only lipgloss and a faint touch of eyeshadow to emphasise the blue depths of her eyes.

With it, she had found a paler pink silk rose. She tried it against her shoulder, above her ear, finally pinning it into the V of the neckline. The final touch was a pair of shoes in a deeper pink, elegant and classic.

Surveying herself in the mirror, it was hard to keep down the touch of excitement. She looked, she thought flatly, better than she ever had before. Young, yet not childish; the smooth, classic lines of the dress gave her some sophistication. It was a pity that the clothes symbolised the worst sort of servitude to her, the bonds of other people's expectations.

A tap on the door heralded Mrs Scrivener. 'Lovely, Cressida,' she said generously. 'I would never have thought that particular shade would have suited you, but it's perfect. You have such beautiful skin. May I suggest just one thing?'

Cressida looked the length of her body. 'Yes, of course.'

'I have a string of pearls which would look spectacular. Come with me and try them on, see what you think.'

They did look spectacular, a long triple strand, ivory against her pale gold skin. In Mrs Scrivener's green and pink bedroom Cressida looked at her reflection once more and said on a sigh, 'Yes, you were right. That's what's needed.'

'Then wear them.' She forestalled Cressida's instinctive protest by saying earnestly, 'My dear, you have no idea how much fun it is having another woman in the house with me. When Sally lived at home we used to have such great times, swapping clothes and plundering each other's bits and pieces. I love Luke dearly, and he's always so appreciative of what I wear, but it's not the same! Do let me lend these to you for tonight.'

Cressida gave in gracefully, smiling to hide the tremor in her lips as she said, 'You're so kind. Thank you.'

Mrs Scrivener said gaily, 'Well, that's settled! Let's go down now.'

Knowing that she looked good gave Cressida confidence to meet Luke's eyes in the drawing-room, responding naturally even though the strange glitter that turned them green shook her; it gave her the poise to deal pleasantly with the older of the two guests, a man in his late twenties who sent one dazzled look her way and was obviously smitten. It was exciting to know that she could have that effect on a man even though she was very wary; once more she realised how circumscribed her life had been. Most women of eighteen had had years to become accustomed to men who flirted with them.

Perhaps the knowledge that she looked good went to her head. Perhaps she preened too obviously, because she didn't know what else she had done to deserve the cool condemnation that sparked like flint in Luke's eyes towards the end of dinner. It made her lose the thread of the conversation she was having with the man beside her. Angry, because Luke had no right to condemn her and it was stupid to be so aware of him, Cressida bit her lip and tried to concentrate harder. So she listened to her neighbour with a feigned interest which soon became real as he told her of the patient, painstaking work entailed in compiling a register of archaeological sites in Northland.

And if, as a kind of counterpoint to the serious conversation, he sent her long looks and smiles which had little to do with the subject—well, she responded to them too, using defiance as a shield against the man who sat at the end of the table, his strong-boned face impassive, but disapproval emanating from him in waves.

Mrs Scrivener asked a question; courteously, her partner turned away from Cressida to answer, and the conversation became general once more.

But Cressida made sure that she did not look at Luke, not then, not later; and when their visitors had left she ran up the stairs to her room so that she didn't have to meet the cold crystal of his gaze.

Still avoiding him, she came down late to breakfast the next morning, but Luke had left early for a sale of pedigreed cattle some miles away. Half disappointed, half relieved, Cressida ate toast and drank orange juice, carefully blanking out any but the most commonplace thoughts. It took such an effort that she didn't hear anything out of the usual until Marie appeared at the door, saying, 'Mr Sandison is here, wanting to know if you'd like to go with them to look for Maori gardens.'

'Oh.' Lost for a response, Cressida stared at her. Then she said uncertainly, 'I—I' would like to go. I'll go and tell Mrs Scrivener, shall I?'

'I'll pack you some lunch,' Marie said practically, adding, 'I know these men with a mission. They stop when it's dark!'

Mrs Scrivener looked doubtful, but after a moment her face cleared and she smiled rather mischievously. 'How nice of them. Of course you must go. Rob Sandison is the son of an old friend of mine, a very nice chap. He'll take care of you. I'd take a jacket if I were you, it can get quite cold by the sea at this time of the year.'

So Cressida found an old anorak and her gumboots before fleeing out to the Land Rover which waited patiently at the front door, arriving just as Marie emerged with a hamper big enough to contain food for the proverbial army.

Rob Sandison greeted Marie with enthusiasm and Cressida with delight, and she felt her spirits lift in the warmth of his uncomplicated admiration.

The day that followed was fascinating. They plotted various *pa* sites, drove all over the station using the network of farm roads with frequent deviations across country, climbed hills the Land Rover couldn't tackle and showed her how they went about their work, using surveyor's techniques to pinpoint each site on a large-scale map of the area.

In between, they laughed and teased her and each other, ate Marie's packed lunch with loud and enthusiastic praise, and stopped twice in sheltered places for coffee: Rob Sandison made it quite obvious that he was attracted to Cressida but it was clear that he had no intention of pushing himself forward. It was the first time in her life that Cressida had been out with two men she didn't know, and perhaps she was a little high on their very masculine appreciation, because as they were bumping back to the homestead in the fading light she thought she had seldom enjoyed a day more.

So it was a pity that the first person she saw when she walked into the homestead after shedding her jacket and boots was Luke. Luke, who stood poised to strike, looking at her with flat savage eyes, dangerous eyes, the only movement in his lean body a muscle flicking beside his mouth.

Cressida froze. She tasted the coppery tang of danger on her tongue, primitive, inescapable.

'What's the matter?' The question had to be forced through muscles tight with strain; she could feel them working in her throat, and saw with a frisson of fear that his burning gaze was fixed on the vulnerable movement.

'Nothing.'

He was lying. She took an uncertain step towards him, but stopped when that deadly stare lifted back to her face.

'Luke?' she breathed.

He kept her pinned, held in stasis by the intensity of that gaze, yet she could not see through it. He revealed no emotion beyond fury, and even as she watched, fascinated and fearful, he mastered that. The red glare faded, was extinguished, and in its place was an icy remoteness, a withdrawal so complete that she shivered.

'You're cold,' he observed aloofly. 'You'd better shower before you come down.'

She recognised this technique. Her father had been an expert at it, using his chilly withdrawal as a method of punishment for day after weary day. But Cressida had no need to cower before it any more. Anger blazed to life, warming her, freeing her from the fear which had kept her silent. Before she had time to think she demanded harshly, 'Why are you angry with me? What have I done?'

Again he said, 'Nothing,' and again he lied.

She bored in for the attack. 'Then you looked at me as though I was something you wouldn't wipe your feet on just for fun? Because it amused you?'

'I've seldom been less amused.'

The level statement was a warning, one she ignored, sweeping on in a bitter torrent of words and emotion, mostly directed at her father, 'Then what *is* the matter with you? Why are you sulking?'

That childish little word might have been a bomb, for the effect it had. Luke's face darkened and she stepped back, aware too late that she had been stupidly provocative. It was as if the restraint which had seemed so vital a part of him had been breached and banished by her careless words. The very contours of his face altered so that it was the Viking who stood before her, lean strong body braced and waiting, his eyes blazing like molten gold as he reached out and pulled her into the hard, fierce tension of his body.

'I discovered,' he said, 'that I didn't like the idea of you stretching your fledgling wings in anyone's company but mine.'

And when Cressida said indignantly, 'I don't know what you m——' he stopped her by the simple expedient of covering her mouth with his.

CHAPTER SIX

IT WAS not the first time Cressida had been kissed. In spite of her father's restrictions, there had been a few others, but at the touch of Luke's mouth the memory of them disappeared. She was so astounded at what was happening that for the first few seconds she just froze, neither resisting nor welcoming the rough expertise of his mouth as it took hers. By the time she had woken up to the danger it was too late; he had made himself master of her responses in a way that was entirely new to her.

It was not so much the feel of his mouth on hers, desperately exciting though that was. It was not even the taste of him, or his scent, warm and male and aroused; it was not the feel of his body, overpowering as it tightened against her, enfolding her, almost crushing her in a sort of desperation which she had never before encountered. What sent a pang of febrile excitement through her was her own incandescent reaction, and the knowledge that somehow she had sent him over a border he had vowed not to cross.

She knew that he had not intended to kiss her, that he had promised himself he would keep his distance; she knew, and she gloried, exulted in the knowledge that for once Luke was unable to exercise his usual control over his emotions.

She should have been angry, even terrified. Perhaps she was, because he was not handling her as the inexperienced girl he knew her to be. He kissed her as though she was his possession, known only to him, bone

127

of his bone and flesh of his flesh, her responses his for the taking, his mouth ardent and cruel and seeking as though he had been jolted over the edge into madness.

Afterwards, she wondered if she should have tried to fight him. Perhaps it would have been better for her self-respect if she had struggled, but her brain sent no such instructions; as if this was what she had been born for, she melted into him, one arm flung about his neck, the other trapped against her side by his, offering him far more than she realised.

At first he was almost brutal, masking his need with a savage bitterness, but her willing response gentled the primitive assault, and soon he was showing her just how many ways there were to be kissed. Tender kisses, gentle as a moth's touch, long, slow kisses, deep, deep kisses when he thrust into the sweet reaches of her mouth in a wildly erotic mimicry of the ultimate embrace, so that she moaned, a haunting little sound torn from her throat by the unexpectedness of it, the elemental sorcery of his desire and her response.

And he showed her how easy it was to become lost in the jungles of passion until her whole being was turned inwards on to the untried, fascinated reactions of her body. Cressida thought dimly that her senses were at once enhanced and muffled; sharpened unbearably by desire, yet she could taste and smell and see only him, her skin heating at the slow slide of his mouth over the long arc of her throat, her brain clouded with the fumes of passion. She was engulfed by him, she had been taken over, made a part of him, but at the same time she had never felt so attuned to herself, to the body she had inhabited for eighteen years and never appreciated until now.

Then Luke lifted his head, and into the drawn darkness of his face there came anger and a bitter acceptance.

'Someone's coming,' he said flatly.

Cressida stared at him, her mouth full and tender as a rose, and he shook her slightly. Something frightening flicked in his eyes as the blaze in them died and was replaced by a bleak whiplash of scorn.

'Pull yourself together,' he commanded, setting her away from him.

How Cressida managed it she never knew, but by the time Mrs Scrivener entered the room she was following his lead, listening with every appearance of interest while he told her of an amusing incident at the sale he had attended that day. However, she could suffer her hostess's keen glance for only a short time, taking the first opportunity to make her escape on the excuse of needing to change.

In her room, she gazed for a long moment at her reflection, her tranced stare travelling from the betraying crushed satin of her mouth to her cheeks, their colour only now fading, and thence to her eyes, their blue depths tormented by forbidden knowledge. She gave a little gasp, understanding at last the look of agonised ecstasy she had seen on Paula Radford's face.

When she came downstairs it was with her features carefully composed into tranquillity. Her strength of will surprised her, but it was all she had to support her pride. The reason for Luke's behaviour was a mystery, but she had not misunderstood that contempt. It was very important not to reveal just how much it had wounded her.

After one piercing look her way, Luke's easy sophistication cast a cloak of courtesy over an evening which could have been spectacularly awkward. Cressida followed his example as best she could, but was wholly relieved when shortly after dinner he left them to go to the study.

With Mrs Scrivener she watched a documentary on

television, welcoming the somewhat sordid subject as an antidote to the bewilderment that racked her brain. After that, she practised typing in her room for an hour or so, then came down to drink tea with her hostess, chatting serenely about her pleasant day with the two archaeologists. When Luke came in she felt her whole body stiffen, like a deer in the presence of a tiger, but she obeyed Mrs Scrivener's injunctions to pour him a cup of tea; if either noticed that she was almost desperately careful not to let her fingers touch his and that she never once looked straight at him, neither of them mentioned it.

But she was jerked out of her careful caution when Luke remarked, 'I've just had a ring from the yacht broker, Cressida. He has a buyer for the *Windhover*.'

'Oh.' Harried, her gaze met eyes remote yet as hard as quartz, and she bit her lip as her lashes fell in something between shame and bewilderment. She hurried on, 'When are they coming to see it?'

'Tomorrow.' He was watching her with uncommon keenness, making no attempt to hide it. 'Do you want to go with them?'

She returned docilely, 'Do you think I should?'

'Not if you don't want to.'

Cressida hadn't been on the *Windhover* since she and Luke had consigned her father's ashes to the waters. With a passion she knew was a little unbalanced, she wanted nothing more to do with the yacht which had come to represent a prison to her.

Crisply, Luke pre-empted any further fretting. 'There's no need for you to go out with them—the broker is well clued up.'

She should have told him that the decision was hers to make, but she didn't. All she wanted to do was get away before she made a complete fool of herself.

So she gave a colourless agreement and shortly after

that excused herself and went up to her bedroom, wondering how it was that a few minutes could change a person's entire life.

She had been infatuated with Luke before; now she didn't know what she felt for him, but it was a far cry from the adolescent crush of yesterday. By forcing her to face the passion dormant inside her he had changed not only her appreciation of herself, but in some deep irreversible way altered her whole attitude to him. It sounded incredibly trite to feel that a kiss had made her a woman, but when she looked back on the Cressida who had not kissed Luke, it was with a woman's regret for the innocence of her girlhood.

And when she thought of him, when she saw him, it was with the darker, richer sensations of a woman who understood at last that passion could blow apart the standards and inhibitions of a lifetime.

She was almost ready for bed, sitting on the side of it brushing her hair, when there came a tap on her door. Incredibly, she jumped, and a pulse began throbbing high and fast in her throat.

Idiot! she scoffed silently. It won't be him.

But her heart continued to beat like the wings of a trapped bird, and when she opened the door to meet Luke's hooded eyes the frantic throbbing increased almost unbearably.

'Let me in,' he commanded softly. When she made no attempt to obey him, he took her hand from the doorhandle and pushed her gently back into the room, closing the door behind them.

Cressida had pulled on her new dressing-gown, but she blushed as that enigmatic gaze found the painful pulsing of her heartbeat at the slender tanned base of her throat.

'I'm not here to seduce you,' said Luke a little harshly.

She swallowed but retorted, 'I know that!' adding hastily as a sardonic gleam warned her that she wasn't going to like his response, 'What do you want?'

'To apologise.' He smiled, the cynical amusement gone, and said gently, 'I was brutal to you before, and I know I frightened you. I came to tell you that I'm sorry and that it won't happen again.'

Why did a mysterious compound of anger and frustration roil up through her brain? She had to force herself to reply evenly, 'It's all right.'

But her eyes slid away from his and she flinched when his hand lifted her chin. 'Is it?' he said quietly. 'Why won't you look at me?'

She could feel colour crawl across her cheeks, but there was no heat with it. The skin tightened, chilled through and through. In a voice that was childishly gruff she muttered, 'I feel embarrassed.'

His gaze pierced through the veils of speech to the emotion behind it. 'Just because I kissed you? You've been kissed before, Cressida. It's because you wanted me, isn't it? Is it the first time that's happened?'

Embarrassment flooded through her. Crimson, she ducked her head, and his mouth quirked in an odd, sardonic smile. He said softly, 'It happens to all of us. Why should you be immune? The most powerful, primitive urge we know, the blind desire to reproduce, wrapped by civilisation into a prettily decorated package called romantic love, but the present in the parcel is beyond taming with logic or words. It lies in wait, it needs only a trigger to set it free, and it's not pretty. It's fire and wind and ecstasy. Did you shock yourself, Cressida?'

The taunting note in the dark voice brought her head up. Stoutly, she tried to face him down. 'You shocked me! I didn't think you—I mean, you're older, and—

and——'

His eyes were thin slivers of purest glittering green. 'I forget how naïve you are. Didn't you realise that I've been wanting you for weeks?'

The deep monotone hypnotised her. She looked up into his face, watched with fascination as a subtle shift took place there, superimposing on the striking features the unsparing hunger of desire. But this time there was no brutality in the kiss, no anger and pain. And this time she knew what to do, discovered how easy it was to melt into him, her mouth opening with slow seduction beneath his . . .

It was the sweetest ravishment, his mouth warm and seeking, the heated play of his breath on her skin as he found the tender innocence of her temples, the astoundingly erotic lobes of her ears, the gentle obstinate line of her chin. His arms held her to him, not tightly, yet firmly, so that added to the bewildering sensations his mouth wreaked on her were the secret signals of his body, the hardening of muscle and the rapid, suffocating beating of his heart.

A tide of fire wound its way, slow and thick and sweet as honey, through Cressida's body; she felt it in her breasts, aching for an unknown touch. It sensitised her skin so that every small area exposed to him burned and throbbed. It clouded her brain and made her lashes sink over half-closed eyes, and when it was strongest it settled in her loins and the pit of her stomach. Without knowing what she did, she groaned and strained towards him, turning her face into the column of his throat and pressing feverish, untutored kisses against the hot skin.

Drowning in sensation, she thought wildly that if he didn't satisfy the demand which tore at her she might die, burst into flames and shrivel away to ashes . . .

Luke said in a voice she didn't recognise, 'Oh God, I

didn't mean to do this. Cressida, no, I can't—I won't——'

Her breath froze in her lungs. She tried to push away, but his arms tightened, sealing her against him so that for one scorching moment she was welded to him, crushed against the hard strength of his chest, the narrow thrust of hips and urgent masculine need, the iron muscles of his thighs. He held her as if for that moment she was the most necessary part of life, and then he released her and stood back, his expression cooling into a disciplined bleakness that fought and overcame the leaping sparks in his eyes.

Slowly, her trembling hand came up to touch her mouth; she watched him with eyes almost black with emotion, her body aching with a frustrated, bitter acceptance.

He swallowed words she was glad not to hear and said jerkily, 'You've just learned something else. Men can cover their desire with all sorts of lies. I didn't come in here to seduce you, but it wouldn't take much for me to carry you across to the bed and make myself so much master of that beautiful body that you could never look at another man without thinking of me.'

Her voice trembled as much as her hand. 'Why?'

Cynicism wove a thread of weariness through his tone. 'I want you—and now you know that you want me. Together we burn up a bloody conflagration. Physically, bed constitutes the next step.'

Colour burned like fire through the pale gold of her skin. She said angrily, 'You had no right——'

'I know it.' Strangely, for a man so confident Luke seemed to hesitate as though searching for the right words. When he spoke it was slowly, the weariness much more pronounced, and very much at variance with the way he was watching her. 'I didn't intend either of these—incidents. You're a guest in my house and very young. Unfortunately, I've known from the first that we would be very good together, just as you have; it's an instinct. But that's only an excuse.'

Cressida said painfully, 'I'd better go.'

'No.' He made as though to move towards her, and stopped as if he had been struck when she flinched away. The narrowed eyes widened; she saw anger and a kind of pain in them, and felt as though her heart was being wrung.

'No,' he said, with more control this time. All emotion had been swept from his expression; she saw only that forbidding restraint, cold and sharp-edged and immovable as a mountain. 'This is my problem, not yours.'

Sudden sharp antagonism made her say, 'Really? From where I was, it seemed that we both had a problem.'

His smile was cynical, very effectively cutting her short. 'Cressida, almost any reasonably young, reasonably attractive man could make you feel that way. You're ripe for loving and you haven't had the experience to be discriminating. What the hell did your father think he was doing?'

Stung by his patronising attitude, she snapped, 'You make me sound like an idiot!'

'Passion can make fools of us all.' Luke laughed mirthlessly, allowing irony full rein. 'Intriguing, isn't it? All that makes humanity noble, the divine curiosity, the compassion and the search for truth, they all go down the drain at the first touch of desire.'

Cressida moved uncertainly, unable to hide her uneasiness. She didn't want him to talk like that; his cynical view on love made her rebellious and frightened. With a sudden flash of insight, she understood why. She, too, had grown up cynical. Too young to understand the convoluted politics of the only marriage she was familiar with, she had decided that, if that was what love was like, she wanted nothing of it. Love made cages. It might be sweet, but a trap was a trap. Yet in her innermost heart she had hoped that the conclusions she had made were false.

Now she was afraid, because it seemed that her hopes were vain; Luke, too, believed that love was nothing more than a frequently inconvenient instinct to propagate the species.

Something died in her heart. She said quietly, 'I still think it would be better if I went, Luke, before I become a nuisance.'

He lifted his hand to shape the line of her shoulder, a wry smile softening the hard line of his mouth. Almost as if the words were torn from him he said, 'You could never be a nuisance, darling. And you're not leaving Five Mile until you have convinced me that you're capable of looking after yourself.'

Catching fire at such autocratic arrogance, Cressida struck out blindly. 'I'll leave when I want to, and there's nothing you can do to stop me! I'm quite capable of looking after myself. I don't need anyone to watch over me, much less you!'

The smile was transmuted into something much less pleasant, although his mouth still curved upwards at the corners. To Cressida's startled eyes it looked as though he snarled, and she tried to pull back. His hand on her shoulder tightened, jerking her close to the leashed power of his body. She dragged a trembling breath into her lungs, striving to banish the sudden sick fear.

Inexorably, Luke pulled her a little closer, until the tips of her breasts just touched his chest. She stiffened and he looked past her face down to the twin points of contact. Cressida felt her breasts tingle; they seemed to swell and tighten, and to her horror the nipples hardened, thrusting ardently against the soft material of her dressing-gown.

'No?' he mocked in a soft level voice. 'How very naïve you are, sweetheart! Do you like this?'

'No!'

'Then why aren't you stopping me?' His voice was smooth as cream. 'You've just said that you don't need anyone to watch over you. Show me.'

Cressida knew several tricks of defence; for a moment she hesitated, but he laughed deep in his throat and a ferocious anger swept away her scruples; without thinking, she twisted to bring her knee up.

Quick as she was, Luke was quicker. Before she was able to get anywhere near him he had pushed and she was falling through the air, to land with a thud on her backside on the floor, and he was laughing at her. Almost winded, she scrambled to her feet, chagrin and anger combining to form an explosive emotional cocktail. She launched herself at his mocking face, fingers clawed in the classic feminine attack, and he caught her wrists and pulled her into him, holding her with her hands behind her back against the hard arousal of his body.

Gasping, because she felt like bursting into tears of rage and frustration, Cressida bit his shoulder. He swore, then laughed again and transferred her wrists to one hand, using his other to force her chin up. She met his leaping, glinting eyes with implacable resistance, somewhat softened by the tears that made his face blur and waver.

Shaken, the feral glitter dying in her eyes, Luke said, 'I'm sorry, that was a lousy thing to do. Cressida?'

She strained to pull free and he let her go, that disturbing irony not unmixed with an utterly infuriating sympathy in his smile. 'Am I forgiven?' he murmured.

Bitterly resentful, she shrugged, then flushed at her

childish reaction. 'No,' she said defiantly, adding with a touchingly shrewd perception, 'But you don't care, do you? In fact, it would serve your purpose if I never forgave you. What makes men like you and my father think you have the right to control people's lives?'

Luke's dark brows lifted as he scanned her angry face with a sudden arrested look. 'Am I relegated to the same category as your father? I know you resented the fact that he tried to wrap you in cotton wool, but look at things his way, Cressida. He was doing the best he could. I suppose the thought of you alone and with no one to turn to if you needed help filled him with horror, just as it does me. You have a touchingly vulnerable air, and I don't need to tell you what effect that has on a certain type of man, do I?'

Scathingly she retorted, 'My father took me away from boarding school as soon as I was sixteen. I wanted to go to university, but he wouldn't have any of it.'

'Life must have been lonely without your mother. You were all that he had left of a family. I can understand that he wanted you with him, although I think it was short-sighted and selfish of him.'

'He took me away from the sort of life I wanted, and forced me to live his life.'

He came across with silent panther steps to where she had retreated as soon as he let her go. He turned her averted chin and looked down at her. 'Did you hate him so much?'

'I—I—*yes*, damn you! Unnatural, isn't it, to hate my own father?'

Cressida lifted a face irradiated with defiance and almost spat the words at him, hating him because he had forced them out of her, because he was the same sort of man as her father and because she loved him with an intensity she was only then beginning to comprehend.

And, contrary to the old adage, with understanding came fear.

Luke sighed and said unexpectedly, 'Entirely understandable, although I doubt if you have it in you to hate anyone. How are you getting on with the diaries?'

'I haven't done anything more on them,' she returned sullenly. 'I've been practising typing, and—well, I help your mother and Marie a lot.'

'And go roaming the place with archaeologists.' He smiled a little tauntingly at her, but without the unnerving fierceness of before. 'You poor little scrap, your eyes are practically closing by themselves. Go to bed. I'll see you in the morning.'

He managed to make her feel like a rather sweet, vulnerable child. Wistfully she watched him go from beneath lowered lashes, then climbed into bed. Somewhat surprisingly, she slept like a log, waking to a morning that was warm and damp, with low clouds threatening to release their moisture any minute, and a soft wind in from the north.

It was embarrassing to meet Luke over the breakfast table, but he acted with a calm self-possession which almost put her at ease, and by the time he drove off in the Land Rover Cressida had decided to follow his example and pretend that yesterday, with all its shocks, had not happened, although her mind had a disconcerting tendency to swing back and relive those terrifying, exalted moments in his arms.

He arrived back at the homestead late in the afternoon, but waited until before dinner to inform Cressida that the yacht had been sold.

'I see,' she said slowly, not lifting her glance from contemplation of the mineral water in her glass. 'Just—like that.'

She missed the glances exchanged by the two others in

the room. After a moment Luke said easily, 'Yes. Sam Thorburn will do the actual signing up. As soon as it's done, the new owner will come up to collect *Windhover* and take her down to the Bay of Islands for a complete refit. Then he and his wife will take her up to the islands. Fiji, I believe.'

She nodded, fighting the sharp sting of tears. '*Windhover* will be happy. She was built for cruising.'

They were very kind to her that night. They were, she thought wearily, kind people. Oh, Luke was a tyrant, but he was a kind tyrant. And she was in love with him. Perhaps she was more like her mother than she had realised. Perhaps there was a curse on the women of her family so that they fell in love with men they couldn't be happy with.

And perhaps she was making a lot out of nothing. Her mother's life could have been an idyll, for all she knew; she had only childish hunches to tell her otherwise.

Spring progressed, with a lot of backsliding, into summer. At Luke's insistence, Cressida learnt how to sit on a horse and how to drive a tractor. She sat and passed her driver's licence, and got slightly drunk on champagne that night, waking up the next morning with enough of a hangover to make her decide that, delicious as champagne was, any more and it wouldn't have been worth it.

She began to feel quite proud of her typing, and learnt how to make exquisite mousses and soufflés of the mandarins and oranges that ripened in the orchard, and how to candy the thick peel of the ugli, that fruit cruelly named by someone who preferred its close cousin the orange. The shearers came, and Cressida watched with interest and some alarm as their corded arms swung in rhythm all day, taking only minutes to change the fat grey-white sheep into much thinner animals with their pink skin showing through the short wool so that they looked down-at-heel but clean.

It was an odd existence, as though time stood still and enclosed her in a bubble. Luke treated her with the charming affection of an older brother for a much younger sister, and she tried to stifle the hunger that gnawed through her defences whenever she saw him. Sometimes, just before she went to sleep, she embarrassed herself by the fantasies she wove, but she managed to forget them during the day.

Then, one brilliant afternoon, Luke found her watching a perky little bantam hen with the brood of chicks she had been given to hatch, and sat down beside her on the cool dry lawn.

'They're so lovely,' she said gruffly. 'Listen, she has a special little cluck she uses when she talks to them. Just like baby talk!'

Luke smiled down at her. 'Clucky?'

'Ah well, it's the season for it, isn't it? Everywhere I look there are babies. I feel quite left out.'

'You're only a baby yourself,' he said teasingly.

Cressida directed a complicated grimace at him. 'Thank you. Still wet behind the ears, I suppose you'd say.'

'Oddly mature, actually. I've just had a call from Sam.'

She stiffened, then forced herself to relax. 'And?'

'And the *Windhover* is to be signed over tomorrow. I wondered if you'd like a last look at her before they take her down for her refit.'

She looked hesitantly at him. He was sitting with his hands clasped about one bent knee, his expression totally without emotion, except for a challenging gleam in those amber-green eyes, yet she realised that he was giving her a chance to make her peace with her father, and suddenly she wanted very much to do that.

'Yes,' she said simply.

Luke got to his feet and held out his hand. 'I'll get Marie to pack us some lunch and we can take her out. It's a wonderful day to cruise.'

Certainly, the sky was a rich bright blue, but there were high streaks of cirrus cloud forming an elongated web to the north. Luke followed her gaze and said, 'Bad weather on its way. We'll be back before it hits.'

So they took the yacht out into the blue waters of the harbour, then a little later put up the spinnaker and slipped out through the heads to the island off the reef which had caused Cressida so much worry on that nightmare journey in. Now both reef and sea looked peaceful, almost playful, with only a soft white wash to hint at the cruel rocks which lay below the surface.

Dolphins joined them, their wise smiling faces lifting and falling as they surged through the water; Cressida leaned over and talked to them, exclaiming with delight as she saw a baby with its mother, and the protective fierceness of the male, swimming close to them and herding them away from the yacht whenever he thought they came too close.

'He's so protective!' she said, laughing.

Luke looked cynical. 'A few years of feminism isn't going to subdue an instinct as basic as that.'

Cressida wasn't going to spoil their lovely day by arguing or allowing herself to dwell on the implications of that. Turning away before her eyes devoured him, she said lightly, 'Chauvinists, both of you.'

Bare to the waist, he was adjusting his stance to the motion, muscles moving in his strong arms and across the wide expanse of his back as he held the yacht on course. The sun turned his skin to bronze. He had changed into shorts as brief as the ones she wore, but his were old and faded and they clung lovingly to his lean flanks, hiding nothing of the smooth musculature beneath.

He possessed a barbaric male potency, she thought, staring with unseeing eyes at the dolphins. It was not just that he was beautifully made, although that was a part of it. He gladdened her eyes, and through them her other senses, so that she could remember how he tasted on her tongue, and the tactile qualities of the pattern of hair against his smooth skin, his warm erotic scent lingering on in her mind, and the deep catch of desire in his voice as he spoke. Physically he was all that a woman could want.

Part of that heart-stopping attraction was his concentrated air of authority. Like the male dolphin, he was confident in his masculinity; he did not have to prove it to anyone, not even himself. But there were other reasons why Cressida loved him. He was kind and possessed of a rigid integrity, brilliant yet easy to talk to, with a dry, rather sardonic sense of humour which prevented him from taking anything too seriously; when he wanted to be, he was the best companion in the world.

They ate lunch on the single tiny beach on the island, beneath the branches of the pohutukawa trees that swooped down over the creamy sand. Afterwards, she allowed herself to be challenged into the water. Accustomed as she was to the balmy oceans of the tropics, the first moments in this southern sea took her breath away, but within a few minutes she found she rather enjoyed the brisk coolness. She was an excellent swimmer; so was Luke. Together they explored the little bay, then he ordered her out and made her get back into her clothes so that she didn't get cold.

'Don't be bossy!' she protested, rather enjoying the feeling of being protected. Just this once, she thought. It can't be dangerous if I indulge in it just this once.

'Comes of being the oldest in the family.'

She laughed, but obediently lay down in the sun. She wore a shirt, so she didn't put on any suncream, but when she woke up the skin on her back felt a little tight, as though the sun had burnt her through the thin cotton. Quietly, she turned her head, and saw Luke stretched out not too far away, his chest rising and falling as he slept. Cressida watched him, her eyes dreamy and wistful, then a little breeze brought a breath of cold across her skin and she sat up, looking to the north with a frown.

For once, it seemed, Luke's weather sense had let him down. The day had closed in; indeed, even as she sat up a low line of grey shut out the horizon, moving with the fast deadly intensity of a squall.

She opened her mouth, but he woke without her calling his name, sitting up in one lithe, economical movement, with no sign of the usual stretching and yawning.

'I think we'd better go,' she said, nodding her head in the direction of the weather.

His mouth tightened, but he wasted no time in recriminations. Instantly levering himself to his feet, he caught her hand and said bluntly, 'It seems you're fated to go through the heads with a storm at your heels once more.'

'This time,' she said clearly, 'I won't be frightened.'

The lines at the corners of his mouth deepened. For a poignant moment, he searched her upturned face as though he didn't believe her, then he laughed. It was like a challenge flung into the wind and there was more than a hint of daring in his face as he caught her close in a hug. 'That sounds like a declaration of confidence! Thank you. Now, let's get the hell out of here.'

But it was not to be so easy. By the time they had got

out to the yacht they were both drenched by stinging needles of rain, while the wind was howling so angrily it was clear that it would be foolish to attempt to make the harbour.

'We could get there,' said Luke, standing in the cabin and dwarfing it, 'but it might be pushing luck a little too far to try.'

'So what do we do?'

He didn't answer for a moment. His eyes rested on Cressida's calm, upturned face in watchful scrutiny, but when he answered it was in a non-committal voice, almost casually. 'We anchor here in the lee of the island until it's over. These storms usually die as quickly as they come.'

'Right,' she said, listening to the chilling scream of the wind in the rigging. She couldn't stop herself from asking, 'Do you think it will get any worse?'

'I doubt it, although I could be wrong. This is just a squall. It will probably blow until towards dawn. Can you start the generator? You did bring a change of clothes, I hope?'

She smiled, 'I never go out on the water without a change. How about you? You're just as wet as I am.'

'Like you, I've been trained to carry spares. However, I'll stay as I am until I've put another anchor down.'

'Do you want any help?'

'No, I know what to do. Get changed and then make us a cup of coffee, will you? When I come down I'll use the radio to get a message to the homestead. Do you think you could organise some sort of meal for tonight?'

'As we only ate about half of the food Marie packed, I think I could, even if it's only toasted sandwiches,' she told him cheerfully.

Twenty minutes later, when he came down below again, she had changed into jeans and T-shirt and was moving with the ease of complete familiarity around the galley. The kettle simmered on the gas stove, and she had found two blankets in a locker, probably left behind because they were old and thin, and draped them over the edge of the seat in an attempt to air them.

'Good, we may need them later,' Luke commented, and proceeded to strip off his wet clothes.

Cressida's pulses set up a drumming which almost drowned out the sound of the rain, but she said in fairly level voice, 'I dumped my wet gear up in the sail locker in the bows. The water's hot enough for you to have a wash if you want one.'

She half turned her head and caught a glimpse of him naked to the waist. Her mouth went dry. He was like one of the ancient gods, big and dominating and overwhelming, tanned skin smooth and slick over the muscles and ligaments and bones of his torso.

'Thanks,' he said absently, clearly not aware that the sight of his half-clothed body swamped her with a surge of sensation primitive in its strength and force. Keeping her eyes rigidly lowered, she handed him a jug of warm water.

Fortunately, he padded out of the cabin on his way foreward; she could hear him whistling as he went into the minuscule washroom and sluiced off the salt and sweat of the last few minutes. It took a lot of will-power for her to drag her mind away from her images of him as a hunting animal, sleek and dangerous and imbued with a feral, exciting power.

But she did it, forcing herself to spoon coffee into two mugs. Unfortunately it turned out to be so much wasted effort, because when Luke padded back into the cabin again she lost complete control of her brain patterns.

He had changed his wet shorts for a pair of jeans just as old and faded, and every bit as clinging. He wore nothing else. Outside, the rain had doused the sun and so little light came in through the portholes that she had turned on the lamps. In their warm glow his half smile made the bold contours of his face even more striking.

A prisoner of her hunger, Cressida let her eyes slide over the gilded planes and angles, the scrolls of fine hair which patterened his chest in antique masculine lines. Helplessly, because she didn't know what to do to break this dark enchantment of her senses, she said, 'The coffee's ready.'

He knew, of course. Just for a moment something explosive flared in his eyes. Then he clamped down hard on to it and in a voice which was polite and completely lacking in emotion he said, 'Good.'

Cressida fought for some semblance of dignity, passing him the coffee before sitting down on the squab as he moved across to look through one of the portholes at the wild scene outside. After a silence jagged with tension and unspoken thoughts, she said the first thing that came into her head. 'If you'd been alone, you'd have tried to make it home, wouldn't you?'

The wide shoulders lifted in the slightest of shrugs. 'Perhaps,' he said without looking at her. 'I have a tendency towards foolhardiness. My father tried to reason it out of me, then when that didn't work he tried beating it out of me. That didn't work either, so he let me experience the results of my actions. It didn't take me very long to begin to think before I let my delight in danger carry me away.'

Did that explain the story Fiona had told her? Shyly she asked, 'If you hadn't inherited responsibilities, Luke, what would you have done with your life?'

He lifted a quizzical brow at her. 'What makes you think I'd have it any different?'

'Intuition.' She could be bland, too.

Above the rim of his mug, his eyes were true green, amused yet sharp with speculation. He drank deep, then came across to rinse the mug in the tiny sink. 'I might have sailed the oceans like your father.'

'I hadn't realised how many people longed to be like him,' she said a little sadly. It had taken her three weeks to answer the letters of condolence forwarded by his publishers and agent, letters which, almost without fail, referred wistfully to her father's freedom. 'Would you like to marry and bring your children up on a yacht, too?'

He shook his head, still watching her with a cool unsparing intensity. 'No. I need roots, and more of them than can be carried in a yacht. A place to come home to, a place that's mine. I love sailing, and in my green and salad days I'd have given my eye-teeth to roam the world like your father, but I wouldn't have cut myself off from the land as definitely as he did. I have a heritage. And, if offered the choice now, I'd take that heritage over the enchantments of sailing like the Flying Dutchman, on and on around the world.'

'The Flying Dutchman was saved by a woman's love,' murmured Cressida, 'but my mother wasn't able to do it for my father.'

'Perhaps she enjoyed it, too. Children are not always the best judges of their parents' lives,' he said gently.

'I know, but Mother was fiercely homesick, and my father resented it. I think she loved him too much to want to clip his wings, so she gave in. And he accepted her sacrifice.'

'That's just surmise on your part, but he was of a generation when women were expected to give up everything to follow their husbands.'

Luke's voice was clipped, as though the subject was unpleasant for him. Paula, she thought, and was wondering how to get them out of this minefield when he resumed, 'I gather from his books that he was a very self-centred man. Perhaps not entirely selfish, he just couldn't understand that there might be a valid point of view other then his own.'

No longer surprised by his perception, she said in a neutral voice, 'Perhaps,' and put an end to the conversation by finishing her coffee and scrambling to her feet.

'It's stopped raining,' he said 'I'll check that the anchors are holding.'

'And I'll see what I can do with the leftovers.'

In her fantasies, Cressida had wondered how it would be if she and he were truly alone together; she had imagined such a situation often and in wildly romantic detail, but the reality was vastly different. The yacht was cold and a little musty, moving uneasily on a sea only just sheltered from the full force of the wind. There was an edge of elemental danger in the air, partly from their situation, but more because, sliding like lava beneath a volcano, was the fact that they were two people marooned, victims of a sensual tension that smouldered and rimmed even the most innocent look and word with sparks of fire.

Yet they kept it under control. No one, not even Paula, would have found anything to look askance at in their conversation. Together they toasted sandwiches and heated Marie's superb game pie, washed the dishes and then settled down in the small, warm oasis of the cabin to drink more coffee. Soon Luke had Cressida laughing helplessly at his recital of the many and unusual trials he had endured while attempting to train one of his sheepdogs, an amiable animal with a great deal of intelligence and very little common sense, and a knack of doing the strangest things.

Chuckling at his description of how difficult it was to rescue the dog from twenty feet up a marcrocarpa tree, she wailed, 'I don't believe it! Dogs can't climb trees!'

'With an angry goose behind it, a dog can do miracles,' he assured her gravely.

He found a tattered pack of cards and taught her how to play poker, teasing her by complaining that she took all the fun out of it, her face told him everything he wanted to know. But at last he said reluctantly, 'I suppose we'd better get to bed—that's your third yawn in as many minutes! I'll go up and check things.'

If he was giving her time to get into bed, he wasn't away for long enough. She hurried around, pulling out the double bunk and arranging the biggest of the two blankets she had found on it, but he was back in a blast of cold fresh air and rain while she was still in the washroom, cleaning her teeth with her finger.

When she emerged, he was standing beside the bunk looking down at it with a shuttered remoteness.

Cressida said quickly, 'That's not the bunk my father died in. After my mother died, he always had the single one.'

'I wasn't worried about that,' Luke told her. 'My bed at home has been in the family for generations. People have died in it, and some of them were not good deaths. I was merely wondering why you put me in a double bunk. Are you planning on sharing it?'

Colour raced up through her skin, but she met his tormenting gaze square on. 'No, I'm not. I just thought that as you're so big you'll feel more comfortable in that one.'

Luke smiled, oddly gentle. 'You respond so satisfactorily to my teasing, but I shouldn't do it. Sleep well, Cressida.'

'Goodnight,' she said hesitantly, and climbed on to the bunk which had been her home for more years than she cared to recall. Once there, she hauled the blanket around her and hoped Luke would stay long enough in the washroom for her to wriggle out of her jeans. He did, and she was safe under the blanket, eyes closed, when he passed her by.

Restlessly she moved her head, wishing there was a pillow. She stretched out her feet, keeping them beneath the pile of her jeans. It was warm enough now, but she knew that towards morning the temperature could drop alarmingly. A noise above the sound of the rain beating down made her eyes fly open. They met a thick blanketing darkness. Luke had turned off the light and the noise had been him getting into his bunk.

As she had so often done before, Cressida lay listening, keeping an unconscious check on the sounds and motions of the *Windhover* to make sure that all was well, until sleep took her unawares.

CHAPTER SEVEN

THE COLD appeared in Cressida's dreams long before she finally woke to a body shaking beneath the ineffective blanket. For long moments she lay trying to brace herself against the shivers, her brain sluggishly trying to decide where she was. The darkness was thick and disorientating; she was just about to call out when a sound brought her upright. She gave a strangled gasp and put out a hand to ward off the dark form looming over her bunk.

Luke said softly, 'Are you awake?'

Relief brought a flood of deceptive warmth. Cressida nodded, then asked hastily, 'Yes, what's the matter?'

'The matter is that I'm freezing. What about you?'

'Cold,' she admitted in a small voice.

He said briskly, 'Right, this is ridiculous,' and unmindful of her squeak of astonishment bent over and scooped her up, holding her clamped against his wide naked chest.

A few steps brought them to the double bunk; he dropped her on to the mattress and did some quick rearranging of the blankets, managing by some miraculous means not to let in any icy draughts. Then, with the agile grace which seemed so at odds with his size, he slid in beside her.

Cressida stiffened away, because he was wearing only brief underpants and she was scorched by the solid length of him enfolded around her.

'Don't give your modesty free rein,' he advised, yawning as he tucked her against him, her back to him, his chin resting comfortably on the top of her head. 'Go back to sleep.'

She had to stifle a sob of ironic laughter. Here she was, in a situation from her wildest imaginings, in bed with the man she loved, both of them almost naked, and he was unromantically ordering her to go to sleep! At first, tension kept her stiff, but soon she began to relax in the beautiful warmth their bodies were kindling from each other. Against her shoulders Luke's heart thudded solidly; one arm lay lax and heavy across her waist.

At that moment she could have killed him for his lack of interest in her, when all that she wanted, and that with a fervour which should have shocked her, was to be swamped by his strength, open to the invasion of his passion, giving him all that she was and in turn receiving from him his life essence, the power and force of his male need.

It hurt, physically. Desire lanced through her body until she was aching and eager and thirsty for satisfaction. It was agony to lie so still in his arms; the heat of his skin against her was an exquisite pain, the rise and fall of his chest a torment. She wanted such wicked things; her skin flamed in a rush of shame and angry desire as she tried to banish pictures from her mind. It would be so easy. All she had to do was turn and press her open mouth to the smooth bulge of his shoulder and he would know, he would respond.

The taste of blood on her tongue shocked her; she began to breathe slowly and evenly, trying to relax muscles locked in stasis and bring the hurried beat of her heart under control.

'Cressida?'

The word was barely enunciated, but her ears were as tuned and on edge as her other senses, and she heard it.

In a voice that sounded thick and rough she answered, 'Yes?'

'What's the matter?'

She couldn't answer that. How could you say to a man, I want you to take me, to make me yours, because I don't think I can bear it if you don't?

Luke asked gently, 'Are you afraid?'

Afraid she might die if he didn't—— Cressida thrust the thought from her and forced her lips to form words. 'No. Why?'

'You seem very tense.'

Wildly, she retorted, 'I'm not used to sleeping with a man.'

His laughter ruffled her hair. And then, so smoothly that for a moment she couldn't believe the evidence of her senses, the hand on her waist slid up until it rested just below the swell of her breast. Cressida gulped breath into lungs that were aching before she whispered in a frozen little voice, 'What—what are you doing?'

'Teaching you,' he said deeply. 'I've wanted to touch you like this ever since I realised that you were not a boy but a very desirable woman. Shall I stop?'

Unfair, her brain screamed, unfair to put the onus on me, but then his hand inched up and she felt the roughness of his palm cup her breast. Reaction shuddered through her in a wave—hot, uncompromising. In a moment stark with insight, she realised that he was every bit as tense as she; that involuntary shiver had brought her hard against a body made of iron, mighty muscles rigid with control.

A small smile, strangely barbaric in its intensity, old as Eve, curled her mouth, echoed in her voice as she whispered, 'No, don't stop.'

And banished the last remnant of common sense. Cressida was not so innocent that she didn't realise that this intensity of need was rare; if she spurned Luke now she might never again experience it. Besides, she loved him, and she wanted her first experience to be with a man she could respect as well as want.

The delicious sensation of his hand on the softness of her breast made her catch her breath; it was as if the old Cressida had been washed away by the storm, and in her place was a woman hungry for her man. Impulsively, she turned into his embrace and pressed herself against him, kissing the bunched muscles along his jaw with an innocent ardour which would have tried the restraint of a saint.

'For God's sake!' Luke ground out. 'Keep still . . .'

'Why?'

He gave the faintest breath of a laugh. 'Because much more of that and I'll be in no shape to give you the gentle initiation you should have!'

It was fascinating to realise that she could cause such havoc in her self-contained Luke, but she did not want to be his pupil. When they came together it must be as equals, in this if in nothing else. What she wanted was Luke so lost in the throes of passion that he was unable to control the full tempest of his desire.

So she stopped kissing his jaw and lowered her head, tasting with delicate greed along the line of his shoulder, feeling with wicked delight the muscles bunch and tense beneath the hot silk of his skin. And in a slow, sleepy little voice that smoked with sensuality she murmured, 'What do you want me to do, Luke?'

He groaned, his taut frame shaking, then pulled her into him as he crushed her willing mouth in a kiss that speared through her in a shaft of pure pleasure, primitive in its intensity. Her mouth opened; she rediscovered the secret delights of kissing, even though he was too hungry to be subtle.

Perhaps she should have been frightened by the fierce tension of his body, the knowing exploration of his hands, but too many sensations warred for supremacy; when his avid mouth followed his hands she began to shake, little sounds fighting their way through the closed passage of her throat to emerge as pleas. She whispered his name, and other disjointed syllables, while he showed her all the mystery which a man and a woman make together, the shared exultation of two bodies as they approach the magical limits of time and space in a private world for them alone.

Cressida forgot that she had wanted to make him lose that steely control; she forgot everything but the rapturous slide of his mouth over her skin, the exquisite sensation of his touch and the potent, age-old chemistry which weakens at the same time that it provides strength. And, at last, when her body was clamorous with an ancient need, Luke moved over her and she knew the rapture of his possession, the first thrust making her cry out in ecstasy, her voice throbbing as she enclosed and engulfed him, taking him into the potency of her woman's body.

He stopped; she could hear him asking something, but the drumming in her ears made it impossible for her to make out the words. Instead she lifted her hands from his sweat-slicked shoulders and pulled him into her in an action which spoke more loudly than any words.

But still he persisted. 'Are you hurt? Cressida, is it painful?'

'Oh no,' she sighed, and her hips moved in an instinctive counterthrust. 'I think I might die . . .'

He laughed and, as the power of his body gathered to enforce complete possession, he said, not attempting to hide the rough male triumph in the words, 'That I can do something about . . .'

It was painfully ecstatic, it was an agony of need, it was a surrender and a victory, it was as though she was ripped from the safe foundations of her character, and yet she had never felt more like Cressida Godwin who had been born to do this . . .

And when it was over, when Luke had gasped her name into her mouth and shuddered and collapsed on to her in exhaustion, she kissed the wet locks of his hair and knew dreamily that she held in her arms all that made her life worthwhile.

When she woke again, the wind and the rain had died and the *Windhover* was lying at rest in the lee of the island, the sun trickling in a golden stream through the hatch opening. Disorientated, her mind still locked into the past, Cressida lay still and quiet, trying to remember where they were.

Her father—she stiffened and turned a slow head. The cabin was empty. Moaning, she turned on to her stomach and pushed her face into her arm, trying to shut out the memories of the night before.

It was impossible; she could find no refuge from them.

The yacht swung, pitched a little, and she knew that Luke had climbed back aboard. Naked under the blanket, she lay crouched and trembling, wishing from the depths of her heart that she had had the sense to get dressed while he was away, instead of indulging in useless repining.

He came padding silently down the companion and over to the bunk; she thought she heard a rueful note in his voice when he observed, 'Hiding your face isn't going to make today go away.'

Damn him! Cressida let his gentle, merciless hands turn her over, and when she looked up she searched his expression for anything but the rather calculating humour which was all that she could read in it.

'You look like an owl,' he said calmly. 'A resentful owl. I've just been out to collect some food. I hope you like oysters for breakfast.'

She nodded, but when he bent over her she couldn't stop herself from stiffening. He jerked upright as the humour fled his expression, leaving it bleak and savage.

'Don't freeze on me now,' he ordered softly, the tone a warning. 'It's too late, Cressida. Last night you gave me everything that I've ever wanted from you, gave it without counting any cost and without looking to the future. I've never had a woman who was as generous and as whole-hearted about it. If you could do that last night, why treat me as though I'm Dracula today?'

The tip of her tongue touched her top lip. She had to swallow because her throat was as dry as a woodchip. 'I must have been out of my head.'

He listened to her stumbling voice with cynical understanding. 'No, you weren't. Thrown off centre, perhaps, but you knew damned well what you wanted.'

Confused and angry, she shook her head. 'I didn't want it,' she cried. 'It just confuses things! And what if I'm pregnant?'

Wide shoulders moved in a slight shrug, magnificently dismissive. 'It might be a little awkward, but we'll just have to get married as soon as possible.'

Cressida sat up, huddling the blanket around shoulders still tender from his rough handling last night. 'Married?' she said in a blank little voice, her eyes widening into infinity.

'Yes, married.' He was watching her with a challenging hardness, the keen edge of his features honed into the kind of determination which permits no opposition.

Her breath hissed softly between her lips. 'I don't want to marry you.'

'Why?'

She cried in an access of anger, 'You haven't even asked me, Luke, you've just told me!'

'And if I ask you, what will you say?'

Danger crackled through the words, wrote itself large in his face, even though the words were barely audible and his face was impassive.

Desperation made her tones pleading. 'You don't want to marry me, Luke. I'm not old enough for you, or sophisticated enough. I don't know what to do—you should marry someone like Paula, someone who knows how to behave as your wife.'

'Paula is nothing to do with us,' he said brusquely.

Because, forced to give up the work that she found such satisfaction in, Paula would not be happy as his wife. So he had looked around for someone young and easily moulded. He hadn't had to look very far: Cressida had been delivered to him on a plate.

Only she was not going to marry him. Her whole being rebelled at the thought of her life with him if she did. She had never been Cressida Godwin, just her father's daughter. If she married Luke, she would be Luke Scrivener's wife. Desired, perhaps loved in a way she would find patronising, she would have no say in her own future: he was so autocratic that he would never see her as anything but the child who had needed rescuing from the storm, and because she loved him she would accept that for a while. But her love would be flawed and resentful, and eventually it might crumble under the weight of his love for another woman. She would be second best. Again.

She would not be able to bear it.

The knowledge was bitter in her mouth, but she said gently enough, 'I'm not going to marry you, Luke.'

'We'll talk about it later,' he said calmly, and bent his

head and kissed her.

How much later did he lift his head and laugh with
satisfaction at her dazzled expression? Only a few
minutes, but she was lying back against the bunk
mattress, her arms wound over his broad back, sighing
her desire into his mouth.

'You'd better get dressed,' he told her, eyes glittering
as he pulled away. 'I told Mother we'd be home fairly
soon.'

His face was clear-cut as a corsair's, filled with the
terrible delight in conquest which can send a man to the
moon or make a petty domestic tyrant of him. The eyes
that rested so possessively on the flushed oval of her face
were ablaze with satisfaction.

Cressida bit her lip until the pain made her wince. Oh,
she made it so easy for him! He didn't even have to use
sex to control her, she was betrayed by her own needs.
Weak, she thought savagely as she watched him walk
across the cabin and up the companionway. Weak and
easily manipulated, that was what she was. He had a
right to that confident aura; he must think she was an
idiot, completely at the mercy of her love.

If love was what it was. She did not even know that.
She had nothing to test it against, no touchstone to
prove that what she felt was not just the adolescent crush
she had assumed it to be at first.

How did one know that love was love?

Not, she thought with a grim determination she did
not recognise in herself, that it mattered. She was not
going to marry him. As she pulled on her clothes and
listened to him moving around outside, she was
surprised at the sense of bleak satisfaction she felt. Luke
could not force her into marriage, and she thought he
was probably too proud to seduce her into it. All she had
to do was refuse to surrender.

And forget as quickly and as totally as she could those blazing, ecstatic moments she had spent with him, the frightening rapture which had shaken her soul. It was sex, she told herself sturdily. Of course it was good with him. That glittering aura of sexuality had more than lived up to its promise; he was extremely gifted. And no doubt a considerable amount of experience had refined the basic talent, she thought snidely, hiding from the sneaking suspicion that her attitude was dirtying what had been a supreme experience.

'Hurry up!'

She reacted to Luke's call with a jump. For a moment she wanted to obey him and race up the companionway, but she forced herself to walk sedately, and there was a steely hue to her eyes which had him eyeing her thoughtfully. However, he made no reference to it, merely observing that with the wind where it was it shouldn't take them long to get home.

She was braced for a confrontation. It was a little lowering that he didn't reopen the subject, but in a way she was pleased. It was going to take all her strength to resist him; she needed a little time to forget how wonderful it had been to lie in his arms before she had to refuse to marry him.

And of course she would have to go.

As they drove up to the homestead she said awkwardly, 'I meant what I said before, Luke.'

'What?' There was a note in his voice that set her nerves jangling. 'The words that came tumbling out last night? You said, if I remember correctly, that you couldn't bear what I was doing to you. Also, I remember you chanting my name as if it was the key to the gates of paradise. Did you mean that, Cressida?'

She bit her lip, recovering enough to say painfully, 'That's below the belt and you know it!'

He slanted her a lop-sided, taunting smile, but his eyes were a cold and knowing green. 'My dearest innocent, haven't you heard that all's fair in love and war?'

This isn't love, Cressida felt like shouting. And I don't want it to be war!

She had no time to say anything more, for they had turned into the garage, and waiting for them in the doorway that led to the rest of the house was Paula, striking as ever in a scarlet skirt and black shirt, her face eager as a child's at Christmas.

Cressida thought she heard the man beside her swear. She said nothing, suddenly so hurt by the pain he must be feeling that she could feel it like an ache in her bones. Not daring to look at him in case she saw his love for Paula written in his face, she barely waited until the Land Rover stopped before jumping out.

But, quick as she was, she still saw the way Paula flung herself into Luke's arms and the words that burst from that passionate mouth. 'Oh, darling, you have to help me! I think I'm pregnant.'

Getting away was actually quite simple. Cressida rang the airport in the nearest town, discovered that the next plane to Auckland left in an hour, and packed her clothes. Mrs Scrivener was in the sitting-room with Luke and Paula, so it was easy enough to carry her bag down to the car her hostess used to get around the district. Then she collected the keys and drove away.

At the tiny airport, she locked the car and took the keys into the office, saying to the attendant, 'Could you ring Five Mile when you're finished here and tell them I got away safely and that you have the keys?'

The attendant was in the throes of getting the small plane's load of passengers processed and boarded; he gave Cressida an absent nod and went on writing. She caught the plane with five minutes to spare.

By the time he had time to think, and realise the oddity of her request, she was well on her way to Auckland.

A motherly American woman sat beside her with her husband. She introduced herself, and when she discovered that Cressida knew even less of the landscape below than she did, took it upon herself to point out the few landmarks she recognised. They were pleasant and kind, and their enthusiastic comments about their holiday stopped Cressida from dwelling on the bitter wasteland that had become her life.

When they arrived at Auckland Airport they insisted on giving her a ride into the city in their taxi. They even suggested she stay at the small hotel they were going to; it was not luxurious, but it was comfortable, and Cressida agreed. That night, she went with them to a small restaurant not too far away and ate quite well. She was rather pleased with herself in a distant kind of way. Remembering that she had felt rather like this her first weeks at Five Mile, she deduced that she was suffering from shock.

Tomorrow, she thought as she sat in the impersonal bedroom, tomorrow she would have to go to see Sam Thorburn, because she had used much of her ready money to buy the airline ticket.

For a long time she sat on the bed, aware that she was shivering, yet not really cold. Outside, the noises of the city seeped in: the sound of traffic, an occasional horn, the warble of an ambulance. It seemed very bleak and cold and impersonal. She wondered if she was going to have difficulty sleeping, but when at last she crawled into bed she went out as if she had been pole-axed, sleeping so heavily that she woke the next morning with a headache.

It went after she had forced herself to swallow coffee. She settled her bill and asked the clerk if she could store her suitcase until she had organised herself. The girl said that that would be perfectly all right, so Cressida waited until nine o'clock to put a call through to the lawyer's office.

His receptionist was helpful and fitted in an appointment later that morning. Numbly, Cressida hung up the receiver, picked up her bag and went out into the street. A little way from the hotel there was a bus stop. She asked a waiting woman if that bus took her into the city. Like everyone she had met, the woman was obliging and friendly; after she had answered Cressida's questions, she asked diffidently, 'I'm sorry for asking, but should you be up? You don't look well.'

Cressida replied, 'I'm all right.' She knew her eyes were flat and dead; she hadn't realised that the rest of her face gave even more away. She summoned a painful smile, hoping it would reassure the woman.

'If it's 'flu, I'd go back to bed if I were you. The one that hit us this year has been a devil for hanging on and reappearing.'

Because she looked so concerned, Cressida said, 'I have go into the city, but perhaps when I come back I'll do that. Thank you.'

It was obvious that her kindly mentor wasn't particularly satisfied with this, but the bus appeared just then and, as it was full and they could not sit together, she had to accept it.

Auckland was saved from banality by its superb situation on a great harbour which seemed inextricably intertwined with the city, so that wherever one looked one caught a glimpse of the sea. Today the waters lay muted beneath a sky of high thin cloud, opal and silver, so scattered with islands that it was impossible to tell which was the mainland and which was not. Normally Cressida would have enjoyed the view. This time she merely stared from the windows of the bus with dull eyes, seeing but not appreciating.

The people in the streets were casually dressed, and there were many Polynesians, as at home as they had been in their tropical islands. They gave the streets an exotic air, exciting and different. Cressida remembered reading somewhere that Auckland was the biggest Polynesian city in the world. She wondered whether they ever regretted exchanging their warm spice-smelling islands for the crisp freshness of New Zealand.

It wasn't difficult to find Sam Thorburn's office, and she was protected by the numbness which dragged at her from being surprised by its size and sophistication. The receptionist smiled and suggested that she wait in one of the pale leather chairs. A few minutes passed and then Sam came through a door, his pleasant face perturbed. As, valiantly smiling, she got to her feet, Cressida saw a flash of relief quickly hidden by a firm impassive expression.

'My dear,' he said warmly, taking her cold hands in his. 'Come on in.'

To her horror, she felt tears chase themselves down her cheeks. Sam responded with speed and dispatch. Within a few seconds she was seated inside his office, a handkerchief thrust into her hand and a cup of coffee ordered on the intercom. He made a few soothing noises, but had the sense to let her cry; Cressida hated the weakness that stopped her regaining control, but when at last the tears dried she felt worse then ever. Sam poured two cups of coffee and drank his with an enthusiasm which brought a gleam of amusement struggling to her wan face.

'I'm sorry,' she said, trying hard to infuse some

strength into her voice.

'I'm not. I'm very glad you came here,' he said fervently. 'Now, I don't think you need to talk to me. Finish your coffee while I make some arrangements.'

She almost spilled the coffee, but although her hand shook she said flatly, 'I don't want you contacting—anyone at Five Mile.'

He gave her a long hard look. 'Are you sure?'

She nodded. After a tense moment he said, 'Very well, then. Wait here.'

He didn't close the door completely behind him, so Cressida could hear the sound of his voice as he gave some crisp instructions to the receptionist. The woman said something in return. There was a pause, then he rapped out a sentence, reappearing immediately with a slight frown between his brows.

'I'm going to take you home,' he told her, cutting off her objection with a shake of his head. 'No, Angie won't mind. At the moment, you're overwrought and exhausted and in no fit state to make any sort of decision. You need a quiet day to think. Tomorrow is soon enough to talk.'

Wearily she said, 'But you can't just take me home like a kitten you've picked up in an alley.'

'Watch me!'

Because it was easier, Cressida gave up protesting and went meekly enough. Reaction was setting in and she was shivering under great waves of exhaustion that prevented her from rational thought. It wasn't until Sam asked her about luggage that she remembered the suitcase she had left at the hotel.

Angie was a vivacious redhead, not beautiful but with superb skin and a sweet seriousness in her expression which made Sam's patent adoration immediately understandable. She took one look at Cressida and said warmly, 'You need a bath, right? Come this way.'

Cressida seemed to have lost all volition. Obediently, she followed her hostess into a bathroom, compliantly divested herself of clothes and got into the bath. A long time later, when Angie tapped on the door and called, she climbed out and dried herself before pulling on the dressing-gown her hostess had hung on a hook behind the door.

Outside, Angie scanned the listless figure before her before saying firmly, 'Food.'

So Cressida ate an omelette, toyed with some salad and swallowed a cup of tea.

'Sleeping pill,' Angie said, handing it to her with a glass of water.

A little spark of resistance in the bruised blue depths of Cressida's eyes was banished with gentle persuasion. 'Trust me. If it's a broken heart, there's nothing like a long sleep to put everything into perspective.'

Like a good child, Cressida swallowed the tablet, then followed her hostess into a chaste bedroom.

And then it was morning and she was sitting up in the bed, with a nasty dryness in her mouth and an incipient headache.

Still lost in the fog of grief and fatigue that insulated her from any emotion stronger than a dull despair, she washed and dressed and brushed her hair. She felt marginally better, and as she followed her nose to the kitchen she pinned on a smile like a banner.

But when she saw who waited for her at the kitchen table the smile vanished and she directed a look of burning reproach at a very uncomfortable Sam.

'Don't blame Sam,' Luke observed pleasantly. 'He knew I'd tear him apart if he hid you.'

He was bitterly, ferociously angry, fury glowing like coals in the brilliance of his eyes. Without waiting for a reply, he got to his feet and continued evenly, 'Now, if we can just use your study, Sam?'

'Cressida needs something to eat. I'll bring along a boiled egg and some toast,' Angie said very firmly. 'In the meantime, Cressida, here's a cup of tea.'

Because there didn't seem anything else she could do, Cressida accepted the proffered tea, but her hand shook as she preceded Luke along the hall and into a pleasantly bookish study.

Once they were seated, he seemed in no hurry to begin. He stood with his back to her, staring out of the window until Cressida's nervousness had impelled her to drink almost all the tea.

Then he turned and regarded her from beneath heavy lids before saying in flat tones, 'Paula is not having my baby. She doesn't even know if she is pregnant, but there is that possibility. She's been having an affair with one of the partners in the firm where she works, and she didn't know what to do, so she came to me for help.'

In a stunned little voice, Cressida said, 'But I thought you were——'

'It's been some time since we saw each other in that light.' Luke paused, but when Cressida made no attempt to finish her remark he began again, this time impatiently. 'Does that make any difference to your feelings?'

Cressida shook her head, staring hopelessly into her cup. 'No,' she whispered at last. 'I'm sorry I behaved so badly, but I can't go back with you.'

Silence stretched so long that she looked up, into a face that was rigid with control; straight line of mouth, eyebrows black bars above eyes that were narrowed to slivers. Stark cheekbones, a straight slash of jawbone and square chin; he looked like some pagan of old, carved in dark wood above a primitive altar.

Cressida drew a deep, terrified breath, and Luke moved away as though he could not bear the sight of her. When he turned back, he was Luke once more, still angry but with that frightening stillness gone. He said in a hard tight voice, 'Why?'

Cressida bit her lips until they were white. Strangely enough, she did not think of denying him. Perhaps she knew that in this she owed him an explanation. 'Because you stifle me,' she said at last, too exhausted to choose her words carefully. 'You treat me as my father did—as though I'm an idiot, someone you can manipulate or intimidate into doing what you want. To him, I was his crew. If I married you, I'd be your wife. I'm not going to let my life go by default to someone who sees me as an object. I am Cressida, but I've never been able to find out who she is.'

He was watching her as though he had never seen her before, his whole aspect arrested. After a moment he said, 'I see. Very well, then. You can stay——'

Cressida interrupted fiercely, 'I don't need your permission, damn you!'

As if her defiance breached the bonds of his control, she found herself whirled into his arms. His mouth branded her in a kiss as cruel as sin, thrusting through the barriers she set in his path until she was gasping, and then she was no longer resisting, but kissing him back with a like savagery, her small teeth sinking into his lip, her body pressed mindlessly, lasciviously, against the corded strength of his.

Then she was free, and they were staring at each other. Through a maelstrom of emotions Cressida sensed that for the first time they spoke together as equals. Luke said in a dry, bleak voice, 'I could force you to come with me.'

She shivered, but her voice was steady as she replied,

'I won't let you use my own body as a weapon against me. It's despicable!'

Irony curled his mouth in a mirthless smile. 'Of course it is. So I'll let you go free. Will you do one thing for me? Angie has a friend who needs a flatmate. Will you live with her until you know your way around?'

Cautiously she nodded, pain clouding her eyes as she realised that this was probably the last time she would see him. The temptation to surrender clawed at her; she asked suddenly, 'Are you in love with Paula?'

'Oh, yes,' he said sardonically, watching her with pitiless eyes.

CHAPTER EIGHT

JAN JAMES was twenty-eight, redheaded, and world-weary, with a wry sense of humour and an inbuilt respect for privacy, her own and others'. Within a fortnight of leaving Five Mile, Cressida was ensconced in her flat in Mount Eden, one of Auckland's leafier suburbs; a week after that she had found herself a temporary job in a flower shop in one of the big hotels in Auckland and was looking forward to extending her skills and earning her first pay packet.

Her boss was an extremely plain woman who told her frankly that she was there because she looked good.

'Class,' she pronounced, exaggerating the noun. 'The customers expect it and you've got it. My daughter finishes her apprenticeship in January, but you have the job till then.'

This suited Cressida perfectly. The academic year began at the beginning of February, and she had already made enquiries about going to technical college. Both Sam and Jan seemed to think that, with her excellent marks, she would have no difficulty getting a place; she decided she would like to learn something about computers.

In the meantime, she had work to fill up the long empty hours of each day. Fortunately, in spite of a secret dread that she might fail, Cressida lived up to expectations. In between serving an international and demanding set of customers, she learned the basics of what was to be a lifelong hobby. It was hard work; she

171

woke up at an ungodly hour to get to the markets so that she could learn how to buy, and sometimes it was late in the evening when she left for home, but that was all to the good. While she was busy in the shop, she didn't have time to think.

And when she arrived back at the flat, so tired that she could hardly say goodnight to Jan—well, that was good too, because then she could fall into bed and sleep as though she had been hit on the head, so she didn't have time to mourn her lost love, or wonder if she had been too stupid in sticking to her guns.

The day she started work she discovered that she was not pregnant. For some atavistic reason it hurt a little, but from then on she concentrated on putting all thoughts of Luke away from her. Succeeded quite well too, she thought.

'You're not eating enough,' Jan told her abruptly one Saturday afternoon. 'You have to be in love.'

Cressida shrugged. 'It will pass.'

'It always does.' Jan contemplated this for a few minutes before saying, 'Oafs!'

'What?'

'Oafs, all of them,' Jan enlarged generously. 'The men we fall in love with who don't love us. Oafs.'

Cressida smiled wryly, but made no reply. That morning, Sam had arrived with a box which held her father's diaries. There was also a letter from his publisher, suggesting that she should send them on so that they could see what could be done with them.

And she had gone through that box with singleminded insistence looking, she was appalled to realise, for a note—*anything*—from Luke.

So she said now, 'And we're idiots.'

'Oh, too true.' Jan got up to wander across the room, eyeing the pretty suburban outlook with gloom. 'Do you want to come to a party tonight? I'm between oafs and I promised to bring a friend. It'll do you good to get out. You're looking pasty and bruised under the eyes, sure sign of a bout of self-pity.'

That marked the beginning of Cressida's social life. To her surprise, she found she enjoyed it. She liked most of the people she came in contact with, enjoyed going out to dinner and the theatre, to parties and the innumerable places there were about the city for outdoor pursuits. And she soon discovered which men wanted more of her than she could give and gave them a clear berth.

If anyone had asked her, she would have said she was happy, and believed it.

Then one night she woke weeping and trembling from a dream, and knew that she had not managed to overcome her desire for Luke; she had merely filled her days and nights with trivialities and refused to face the fact that he had taken her heart with him when he went back to Five Mile.

As she sat on the edge of her narrow bed, sipping the milk she had heated for herself, her eyes fell on the box containing her father's diaries. Some compulsion took her across the room; she opened the lid and stood for a long moment, looking down at the books. Her hand came out to tentatively stroke the cover of the topmost one; she whispered, 'Oh God, what shall I do?' and shut the box as if its contents were unclean.

But in the morning she knew she was going to have to finish setting the diaries in order.

So her full days became even fuller, until Jan frowned and muttered and complained because Cressida had permanent dark shadows under her eyes.

'I have to get this done,' Cressida explained tiredly. She looked down at the typewriter she had hired, saying in a drained voice, 'It's funny, isn't it? You can live with someone all your life and never know them.'

'Your father?'

'Yes.'

'Parents are weird, anyway,' Jan said gloomily. Her head lifted at the shrill ring of the telephone. 'I just hope that's not mine.'

Cressida grinned. Jan complained a lot about her parents, but had once admitted that the reason she didn't live at home was because she and her mother were too alike.

'Cress, it's for you.'

It was Mrs Scrivener, the tinny quality of the line failing to hide the anguish in her voice. 'Cressida, Luke's been hurt in an accident. He's been flown down to Whangarei Base Hospital.'

'I'll get there as soon as I can.' Did she have to make a decision? She never knew. Cold terror made her a spectator as she heard her voice making crisp, competent plans, contacting her employer to explain her absence, ordering a taxi to take her out to the airport to the plane she had hired to take her to Whangarei.

Then she sat like stone, remembering another small plane, another trip to Whangarei. Beneath the golden skin, her features were drawn and agonised.

It didn't take much more than forty minutes to get to the little city on its long harbour. Cressida picked up the hire car at the airport and drove carefully to the hospital. But in the car park she sat long moments striving for control, her blank eyes fixed on the faceless windows in the hospital building. Was Luke fighting for his life behind one of them, that beautiful body broken on the rack of pain?

At reception they told her he was in Intensive Care, and showed her how to get there. Cressida went up in the lift and through the doors to where Mrs Scrivener sat beside her son, who lay wired up to machinery like a robot, all of his splendid primeval vitality extinguished like a snuffed candle.

Cressida drew a sharp, anguished breath, but her voice was steady as she asked, 'How is he?'

Instantly Luke's eyelids lifted, the lashes fluttering a second before they slid slowly down, as though the effort was too much. The wide mouth parted. His hand turned, a movement so small she almost missed it, but she forced back tears at the little groping motion.

She cupped his lax fingers in both her hands, warming their chilled length. 'Yes, I'm here,' she said steadily. 'It's going to be all right, darling. Relax, go to sleep.'

The long fingers eased into slackness; she asked urgently, 'How is he? What happened?'

'The bulldozer crushed him.' Mrs Scrivener wiped her eyes. 'We've had a lot of rain and the culvert at the bottom of the hill collapsed, so Luke took the 'dozer down to fix it. The ground gave way and he was thrown under the machine. He's broken an arm and some ribs, but they say there aren't any internal injuries, thank God.'

'Then why does he look so terrible?'

'It took them over an hour to get him out, and he's in shock.' The ward Sister was coolly professional. 'In situations like that, there's an outpouring of plasma into the injured tissues, which swell and become hard. Blood pressure falls and the patient can go into profound shock. As well, the injured muscles pour poisonous stuff into the bloodstream, which puts a considerable strain on the kidneys. However, Mr Scrivener is not in dire straits, he's strong and a good fighter, and he was in hospital and getting treatment before too much damage was done.' She bestowed a smile of feminine complicity on Cressida. 'Now that you're here, I expect him to get better almost immediately!'

But he looked very ill to the two women who sat with him all that day until they were politely ordered away late in the evening. Mrs Scrivener had booked a room at a motel close by; she and Cressida spent a long, wakeful night there, and after a sketchy breakfast the next morning returned to the hospital.

Neither spoke as they went up in the lift, so that the cool, confident tones of the woman in the foyer were only too audible.

'I tell you, this is ridiculous! He——'

Relief flashed into the face of the nurse who was holding Paula Radford at bay as she looked beyond her and saw the two women step through the lift doors.

'Here are Mrs Scrivener and Miss Godwin,' she said, not without some satisfaction. 'They'll tell you that Mr Scrivener is not allowed any visitors.'

Paula turned, her eyes narrowing as she surveyed Cressida's white face. After a long tense moment she drawled, 'Except, presumably, his mother.'

Sensibly the nurse made no reply. It was Mrs Scrivener who said crisply, 'And Cressida.'

The lovely face hardened as Paula scrutinised Cressida. Beyond that first quick look, her eyes hadn't moved from Cressida's face. She said slowly, 'I'll tell you what—let's both go in, and we'll each say his name. The one he answers can stay.' Her gaze challenged, confident and as sharp as a sword. 'One word isn't likely to set him back.'

'Paula——' Mrs Scrivener began, but Cressida nodded.

'Very well, then,' Paula said triumphantly, almost pushing past the nurse into the ward.

Paula gave a horrified gasp when she saw Luke, pale and still in the high bed. Cressida saw her pallor and the trembling mouth, and realised that the other woman loved him. A sick certainty made her falter. In that moment, she understood the value of what she had lost. Luke had said he loved Paula; he would answer her. What he felt for Cressida was responsibility run mad, and the easy passion of any man for any woman.

Paula came to halt beside the bed, her thin hands gripping each other so tightly that the knuckles were white. 'Luke,' she said.

It took for ever to realise that he made no response. Not a muscle in the drawn face moved. Paula lifted anguished eyes and looked directly at Cressida. One word, she had said, and one word was all that she was going to say.

Cressida swallowed, then said his name almost under her breath.

His black brows twitched into a frown and after a long moment the long lashes moved as they had the day before, only this time he was able to open his eyes properly. She slid into the chair and took his hand, bending to cover his mouth for a second with her own trembling lips, joy lancing like a golden spear through her heart. She didn't even hear Paula go.

But when she lifted her head Luke's eyes were closed once more. He stayed like that, still and apparently unconscious for so long that she began to panic. But even as she looked around for a nurse he opened his eyes again, still frowning.

A tremulous smile pulled at Cressida's nervous mouth. It met with no response. The shimmering green-amber lights had faded from his eyes; they were dull brown. He demanded painfully, 'What the hell are you doing here?'

'I rang her.' Mrs Scrivener was brisk and no-nonsense.

Luke's eyes wandered towards his mother's face. It obviously hurt to talk, but each word was clear and biting as he drawled, 'Silly of you, Mama. Cressida's a big girl now, she has a career. How long have you been here, Cressida?'

She swallowed. 'Since last night.'

'Long enough to convince yourself that I'm on the path to health?'

She nodded, summoning a smile from somewhere, while pain clawed at her heart.

'Then we mustn't keep you here any longer,' he said imperiously. He was still as pale as a wraith, but the hard features revealed nothing but implacable determination.

Gracefully Cressida got to her feet. She must have said something to a worried Mrs Scrivener: she never could recall what it was. But as she left them she heard Luke say far too clearly, 'Did I hear Paula before?'

So Paula had won. Cressida went back to Auckland in the bus, her cold hands folded tightly in her lap, gazing unseeingly out of the window. From that day, she ceased to hope.

Jan was tactful. She made no comment while Cressida worked too many hours over her father's diaries, said nothing when all offers to take her out were politely refused. But the night she came in and found her flatmate sitting at the table in the kitchen, staring into space, with the manuscript finished and ready to go before her, she broke the rules of a lifetime and said crisply, 'OK, that's it. You can tell me why you're trying to imitate the Dying Swan or I'll give you a dose of sulphur every day until you start looking like a human being again!'

Cressida looked at her, saw the genuine concern and worry in her friend's face, and burst into tears. It seemed easier to tell her than resist. Dimly she realised that she was perilously close to surrendering to the ever-present torment that rendered her days grey and her nights long marathons of bitter suffering.

'What sort of man is he?' demanded Jan at the end of the recital, shaken out of her customary placidity. 'Arrogant swine! Oh, I'd like to give him a piece of my mind. Making you fall in love with him and then booting you out——'

The pain which had blocked Cressida's throat ever since she left Luke had eased very slightly. She said with a mirthless little smile, 'I ran away.'

'So I should think! He sounds like the oaf to end all oafs.'

'He's loaded with charm.'

'So? The worst are. What are you going to do now?'

'Nothing,' Cressida said drearily. She pushed at the parcel with her finger. 'There's nothing I can do. He's always loved Paula. It's all right, I'll get over him. People no longer die of unrequited love.'

'No.' But Jan sounded doubtful. She watched that finger, pushing ceaselessly at the pile of manuscript. 'What will you do to fill in your time now you've finished that?'

Cressida didn't answer directly; her eyes, too, fell to the papers in front of her. In a voice flat with exhaustion she said, 'Luke was right when he told me I should do this. It's helped me to understand my father so much better.'

'So you no longer hate him?'

She shook her head. 'He did what he thought was best. One thing I've found out was that my mother made him promise to take me away from the school. She was afraid we would grow apart and that I'd be alone.'

'Instead, she made it almost impossible for you to learn how to live in the world.'

Cressida nodded, her mouth drooping at the corners like a sad clown. 'He would have preferred to sail by himself, but he felt bound by the promise he'd made to my mother. Funny, isn't it? I wasted a lot of time thinking I disliked him, that he was selfish, and all the time he would have been happier if I'd been doing what I wanted to.'

'Parents,' Jan told her wisely, 'are strange kittle-cattle. Now, do you want to come to this party with Richard and me tonight? I need a chaperon; I'm not looking forward to fighting him off afterwards.'

Cressida smiled, because Richard treated Jan as if she were a piece of rare porcelain that might shatter if he breathed too heavily close by. 'No. I'm going to have a bath and then I'm going to bed. I'm sorry to have dumped all my woes on to you.'

'Oh, any time. That's what friends are for. Feel better?'

'Yes.' It was true. Somehow, Jan's matter-of-fact friendship had cracked the crystal cocoon of isolation. Love still burned like an exquisite wound in her heart; but instead of cringing away from its pangs she felt an upwelling of courage. So, she had loved, for all the wrong reasons, and she had lost him—for all the right reasons. That last meeting in the hospital had convinced her that it was Paula Luke loved, Paula he wanted. She hoped they had patched up their differences; above all else, she wanted Luke to have the fulfilment which was not to be for her.

She did not grieve at her decision to refuse him. One thing she had discovered about herself was that she was possessive. Knowing that she came second would have made it impossible for her to live with him; her love was too fierce, as elemental as the sea and the storm. She could accept nothing but a like passion in return.

After Jan left with her adoring Richard, Cressida had her bath. She washed her face and pulled on a yellow nightshirt ready for bed. For half an hour she watched a situation comedy on television, then switched the set off, yawning and ready for bed.

The doorbell brought her up short half-way across the sitting-room. Frowning, because it was late, she went out into the tiny hall and put her eye to the little fish-eye lens. And staggered.

Through the door she heard Luke say laconically, 'If you don't open the door, I'll kick it down.'

Cressida recognised that voice. Reckless, stripped of every tone but concentrated authority, Luke was prepared to take on the world with his bare hands. So she opened the door, looking dumbly up at him as he came through with lithe soundless steps.

Then, 'You're not limping!' she said joyfully.

'No. Neither does it hurt any more when I breathe. I have a complete clearance from the hospital. Tell me, do you make a habit of opening the door to men in that outfit?'

Cressida looked down at her gay cotton nightshirt, so happy that she didn't even try to hide the pleasure in her voice. 'Only,' she said demurely, 'when they threaten to break the door down.'

After directing a narrow-eyed stare at her, Luke strode into the sitting-room, looking around with interest. 'Nice,' he observed, after a moment. 'Aren't you going to offer me something to drink?'

She shook her head. 'Not until you tell me why you're here.'

Something dangerous gleamed in his eyes. 'To take you home, of course. You've had long enough to get your father's diaries finished, and to have a taste of life without me.'

You,' she said with great courage, 'are an arrogant bastard.'

He gave her a tightlipped smile, his eyes hooded. 'Only when something is very important to me.'

Cressida lifted her head, her glance very straight. 'What about Paula?'

He frowned. 'May I sit down?'

Alarmed she said, 'Oh, yes—is your leg hurting you?'

Luke found the biggest chair in the room and lowered himself a little more carefully than usual into it. Even sitting down, he dwarfed the room, his masculine charisma blazing forth unabated.

'It aches a little,' he said casually. He was watching her too closely, his expression sardonically amused at her quick apprehension. Unexpectedly, he went on, 'Paula is—no, Paula *was*. I enjoy her company, and until you appeared on the scene I thought that if I were to marry anyone, she would be the one. But I always knew that she needed her work more than she needed me. Just as I knew that whatever I felt for her was much less than love.' His voice deepened. 'Believe this, if you can believe nothing else. I saw you and I knew that you were what I'd been waiting for. It was as simple as recognition, as elemental as a smile. You pushed your hood back from your head and I saw your grave little face with its passionate mouth and eyes deep enough to swallow my soul, and I felt my heart twist.'

Cressida wanted to believe him—oh, how she wanted to believe him! But she found it difficult to accept that any man could prefer her to Paula. In a low voice she said, 'You didn't show any signs of it.'

'I had some remnants of honour,' he said ironically. 'You were a baby, totally innocent. The last thing you needed was the burden of my love. And I realised very quickly that there was something strange in your relationship with your father. You were in shock, but you were too composed, and sudden alarming sparks of bitterness kept flaring out. I knew I had to wait. It was the hardest thing I've ever done.'

She smiled. 'You ordered me about as if I were a child!'

His mouth quirked in self-derision. 'I had this foolish idea that I might be able to keep my hands off you if I treated you as an extra hand about the place.'

'Did it work?'

'You know it didn't. You responded far too readily to the basic attraction between us, and you had no tricks, no skill at hiding your reactions. And this damned inconvenient passion I had conceived for you grew daily until it was something unmanageable and painful.'

His choice of words startled her, but not as much as the level bitter tone they were delivered in. She said wonderingly, 'Inconvenient?'

Luke leaned back into the chair, hands in his pockets as he surveyed the long length of his legs before him. his voice was reflective, almost cynical, roughened by an undertone which revealed his seriousness. 'I'm sorry if that offends you, but I found it most inconvenient. If, during the years Paula and I were a couple, anyone had asked me about love, I would have told them it was a comfortable amalgam of liking and desire and companionship. I was quite happy to have it so. Then I saw you, a child far too young for me, and I discovered that I'd been unbearably arrogant and smug. Love is wildfire and rapture, pain and exaltation and a savage, possessive desire which scared the hell out of me. It was bloody inconvenient, especially as for all your awareness of me it was painfully obvious that you were indulging in your first adolescent crush.'

Cressida said with difficulty, 'I suppose I am very naïve. You must resent that.'

'I expected—no, I hoped for too much. As for resenting, yes, I did. In a way, I still do.' And, before she could do more than send a wounded look his way, he smiled without humour and held out his hand, arrogant as ever.

Cressida went across to him, the chill that had assailed her at his words banished by the way he pulled her down on to his lap, engulfing her in the warmth she had never stopped missing.

'Pride,' he said in a calm voice belied by the smouldering intensity of his gaze. 'I suppose it's the most devilish emotion in the whole range, and the most insidious. Whole civilizations have been organised to deal with loss of face, people have died for it, killed for it and triumphantly committed atrocities to appease it. Is it any wonder I took refuge in it when my emotions about you grew too unmanageable? After the first time I kissed you I decided I wasn't going to make any more moves until you showed me that you were ready.'

'So you used Paula.' Cressida met his aggressive gaze steadily and told him what she had heard and seen in the library the first weekend that Paula had come to Five Mile. Even remembering that impassioned embrace made her feel sick.

Luke listened, his face impassive, then said bleakly, 'What you saw and heard was her trying to persuade me that marriage would be good for us.'

Cressida's eyes filled with tears. His arms tightened before he continued, 'Yes, it was hard. I'd told her it was over. She had every right to feel disillusioned with me, but there was no way I could tie myself down to a bloodless marriage. I don't blame her for acting a little—out of character.'

'She loves you,' she said in a low voice.

'In a way, but not the right way.' His mouth on her wet lashes was warm and persuasive; it moved down slowly to the corner of her mouth. His tongue touched there, found the curve of her bottom lip and ran slowly, achingly, along it. When he spoke, the words were caught in her mouth. 'She was suffering her own inconvenient passion. He's one of the partners of the firm, and I think she hoped that marriage to me would put an end to it. Instead, she went back and found herself caught up in a full-blown affair; it hurt, because he's married. That was why she came to Five Mile when she thought she might be pregnant. She needed help.'

'So she came to you.'

A note of possessiveness must have threaded its way through her voice, for Luke said quietly, 'Yes. We've known each other since we were children, Cressida. I was the natural person for her to turn to. Are you going to be jealous?'

She stiffened, then buried her head in the warm strength of his throat. 'You said you loved her.'

'I wanted to hurt you.'

'She's so beautiful . . .'

'So are you.'

'. . . and so suitable!'

He said in an arrested voice, 'You're perfect.'

Cressida looked up at him, her eyes wounded, and saw to her astonishment that he was speaking the truth as he saw it.

He said deeply, 'I love you, Cressida. Not because I want to, or decided to, not because you're kind and compassionate and stubborn and fiery, not even because when we made love you took me to paradise, but because I looked at you and I knew that you were mine, and I yours. You aren't ready for me, but it makes no difference. You have the right to grow up, to experience all the things that you've missed. I tried to give you time, but I've discovered that I'm too selfish. Fear does strange things to a man, Cressida. I'm not used to feeling insecure; because of it I behaved despicably. I deliberately seduced you because I hoped I might be able to tie you to me with sex and, perhaps, pregnancy. I'd have scorned any other man who behaved as I did. I felt nothing but contempt for myself, but I took you just the same. Can you forgive me for that?'

'If you can forgive me for running away from you,' she whispered. 'If you can forgive me for confusing you with my father.'

'I'd forgive you anything.' Awed, Cressida realised that he meant it. Her heart leapt in her breast; she kissed the determined line of his mouth tenderly and told him of the discoveries she had made about her father. She finished shyly, 'Working on his diary gave me an entirely different idea of him. He thought that to be a good father he had to protect me; he knew I was resentful, but it only made him surer that I needed guidance. When he died, I felt an overwhelming relief.'

'And guilt,' said Luke quietly.

Startled, she nodded. 'Was it so easy to see? I felt as though, somehow, my yearning to be free of him had killed him. And then I felt doubly guilty, because I couldn't mourn him. His death seemed a release. Everyone expected me to be distraught with grief, and all I could feel was a cold emptiness.'

'Shock,' he said succinctly.

Cressida sighed, loving him so hard that it was an ache inside her. 'Yes, I suppose so. When I read his diaries I realised how self-centred I'd been. I was sick to death of roaming, roaming, roaming, all I wanted was a normal life like everyone else, but Dad loved the sea in a way that was almost mystical; he quite literally felt ill if he was unable to see it. I don't think he did the right thing, but I can see why he did it.'

'That's the first time you've ever called him Dad. Up until now it's been "my father".'

'I know.' She looked sadly up at him, saw him smiling with a wealth of understanding and whispered, 'I do love you. I must have loved him too, because when I fell in love I picked another arrogant, dictatorial autocrat!'

Luke grinned, totally unrepentant, all easy masculine confidence, his eyes gleaming beneath the heavy lashes in a promise of what would come. A surge of delight mixed with the lazy passion flowing through her veins in an erotic, unbearably sweet tide.

But although he must have felt the little shudder she gave he said quietly, 'In a way, when you left me I was almost relieved. I could never have sent you away, but once you were gone I thought I could free myself of the shackles you had set so firmly in place and go back to being the man I was before I met you.'

'But you couldn't,' Cressida said joyously.

The lamp gleamed fire on his head as he shook it. Laughter and a mocking complicity fired his eyes to gold, pure and keen and blazing. 'No. Instead, I discovered that loneliness can eat your heart away. I paid for my greed, my attempted manipulation. But although more than anything I wanted to drag you back home to Five Mile I knew I had to let you find out just how much you wanted me. Love is worth nothing, it's just a commodity, bought and paid for, unless it's offered freely. And that's what I wanted from you, not an unwilling physical attraction, or dependence, or a longing for security. I wanted you to love me.'

As she began to speak, he touched his forefinger to her mouth, silencing her protestation of love. 'And I sent you away from hospital because I didn't want your sympathy. Perhaps I saw a chance to punish you a little for the pain you'd put me through.'

Cressida kissed his finger, her face pale as she remembered. 'You were cruel.'

'Yes.' Luke curved his hands around her face, tilting it so that he could see it. 'I can be cruel. Am I forgiven?'

She could forgive him anything. The rapture that ignited her expression told him that, all of her joy and love blazing forth to transform her. Luke took a deep breath, and it was as though he shook off the shackles of some unbearable constraint. His face hardened into a primitive mask, drawn with desire, and his mouth came down on hers in a kiss as uncompromising as it was masterful.

When he lifted his head she was shaking, her heartbeat threatening to burst through her body; she touched her tongue to her throbbing lips. His mouth tightened. He said harshly, 'Oh God, Cressida, it's been hell, wanting you so much that I ache, and knowing that I couldn't come to you. Tell me you love me.'

Very sweetly she said, 'I love you. I know I'll never regret loving you.'

'Show me,' he whispered.

Her lashes flew up in shock. He was looking at her with such longing that her body clenched in a pang of exquisite desire. For long seconds they stared into each other's eyes, until she said beneath her breath, 'Come with me.'

The bed was narrow, but it would suffice. Cressida stood beside it and watched with eyes which were black with need as Luke came towards her. He stopped just out of reach and said quietly, 'Are you sure, my heart?'

'Oh, yes.' Her voice was uneven, but she held his gaze steadily. 'I don't think I've ever been surer of anything in my whole life.'

'Then come here.'

Afterwards she lay trembling, trying to catch her

breath as the waves of sheer, shocking pleasure slowly ebbed and faded. A yawn caught her unawares; she relaxed, understanding for the first time why cats enjoyed stretching so much. Luke opened eyes that still mirrored the primitive power and extent of the sensations which had carried them beyond the confines of this world. He looked awed and tender and replete with masculine satisfaction. He kissed her throat, and a small mark on her arm, and a tiny mole on her hip, before rolling over on to his back.

'I was not,' he told the ceiling, 'going to do that.'

Cressida laughed. 'I don't recall you saying no!'

His hard mouth softened. He turned his head and fixed her with a pure green gaze. 'Are you going to be happy living with me at Five Mile?'

'I'd be happy living with you anywhere.' The words were a vow.

He searched her face with unsparing intensity, then smiled. 'Good. Because I'm afraid I'm very possessive.'

Cressida laughed again, and came up on one elbow, leaning over him to kiss his mouth with a lazy, confident hunger. 'So,' she said very dulcetly, 'am I. I used to think falling in love was a trap. I didn't want to be caught in it like my mother, unable to get out. But now I know it's a trap that catches both lovers, the sweetest trap in all the world.'

His eyes mocked, but it was a gentle teasing. He caught her chin and brought her face down within reach of his mouth. Against her tender lips he said, 'And the only real freedom, my heart.'

As she surrendered, she knew he was right. Apart, they had been crippled, barely able to function; together, they were complete, free to make the lifelong commitment that was love.

Harlequin Presents

Coming Next Month

1135 A LIFETIME AND BEYOND Alison Fraser
Kelly Cormack had loved her wayward mother, but promised herself never to follow in her footsteps where men are concerned. Then along comes Ryan Devlin, and she realizes she's inherited her mother's talent for loving unwisely....

1136 ONE STOLEN MOMENT Rosemary Hammond
Claudia can never dance again—and without dancing she doesn't want to live. Until artist Julian Graves provokes her to anger and his small daughter inspires her to affection—and suddenly she sees the way ahead. But Julian has problems of his own.

1137 FOR ONE NIGHT Penny Jordan
Diana had made love with a complete stranger after the shock of her best friend's death. When she finds she's pregnant, she makes a fresh start in a new village—only to find that one person there, Marcus Simons, does know her.

1138 JUDGEMENT Madeleine Ker
With just a few words Dominic Raven shatters Honor's sister's chance for a happy marriage. Honor hates him without knowing him. So when he comes to investigate security at Honor's company, sparks are bound to fly!

1139 LORD AND MASTER Joanna Mansell
After two of her clients had been summarily dismissed, Alice sets off for Rossmere Hall to redeem the reputation of her placement agency. However, her problems with Lord Rossmere certainly aren't the ones she's been anticipating.

1140 A QUESTION OF PRIDE Michelle Reid
Deeply in love, Clea gives Max everything he asks for, at work and away from it. Then two bombshells drop into her life that change it irrevocably. Her only concern is—how will Max react?

1141 LAND OF ILLUSION Kay Thorpe
Nicola's whirlwind romance in the Venezuelan jungle leads to marriage with Ross King. In the different world of Hollywood, she barely recognizes the top film director as the man she married. And she isn't sure how Ross feels about his innocent little wife....

1142 MISTAKEN WEDDING Sally Wentworth
In the five years since their bitter quarrel, Carina has avoided contact with Luis, the man who swept her off her feet and into marriage. But when circumstances force her to ask Luis for help, she discovers his attraction is still dangerous!

Available in January wherever paperback books are sold, or through Harlequin Reader Service:

In the U.S.
901 Fuhrmann Blvd.
P.O. Box 1397
Buffalo, N.Y. 14240-1397

In Canada
P.O. Box 603
Fort Erie, Ontario
L2A 5X3

Harlequin Historicals

Step into a world of pulsing adventure, gripping emotion and lush sensuality with these evocative love stories penned by today's best-selling authors in the highest romantic tradition. Pursuing their passionate dreams against a backdrop of the past's most colorful and dramatic moments, our vibrant heroines and dashing heroes will make history come alive for you.

Watch for two new Harlequin Historicals each month, available wherever Harlequin books are sold. History was never so much fun—you won't want to miss a single moment!

GHIST-1